SUZANNE

THE
GREEN
DOG

A MOSTLY True STORY

SCHOLASTIC INC.

New York Toronto London Auckland Sydney
Mexico City New Delhi Hong Kong Buenos Aires

ISBN 0-439-81120-1

Copyright © 2003 by Suzanne Fisher Staples. All rights reserved.
Published by Scholastic Inc., 557 Broadway, New York, NY 10012, by arrangement
with HarperCollins Publishers. SCHOLASTIC and associated logos are trademarks
and/or registered trademarks of Scholastic Inc.

12 11 10 9 8 7 6 5   7 8 9 10/0

Printed in the U.S.A.   40

First Scholastic printing, October 2005

Typography by Amy Ryan

I dedicate this book with love to my family: In memory of my mother, Helen Brittain Fisher, who spent the last year of her life helping me to remember that summer on Chapman Lake; my father, Robert Charles Fisher, whose reputation for being large had as much to do with his heart as his size 14½ shoes; my brother Charles Alan Fisher, who really was all that charming; and to my grandmother Elizabeth Glasser Fisher, who implanted in all of us a love of stories and books; also to my brother Robert and my sister Karen: here's to many more golden summers. With love.

From left to right: Suzanne, Bobby, Charlie, Karen

CONTENTS

GIRL NEEDS DOG

It's the first day of summer—the best day of the year. I awake before the sun, the house still sleeping around me. I sit up and stretch in the chilly semidarkness. My sister lies on the sagging mattress of an iron bed across the room, her plump arms and legs sprawled on top of the covers. I'm freezing—she's too hot. Karen and I couldn't be more different if we tried.

I turn back the flannel sheet and wool blanket in slow motion to keep the springs on my old brass bed from squawking. Karen can sleep until noon if you let her, and she can be as grouchy as a bear with a thorn in its foot if you wake her before she's ready.

I wiggle into last year's bathing suit, which is now too short. Little threads of elastic stick out where the seat has worn thin. Technically, it's still too cold for swimming, but it seems a shame not to celebrate the first day after fourth grade with a swim if it warms up just a little. At the end of each school year we wait for my mother to pronounce the lake warm enough for swimming. She usually does it the first day of vacation, no matter how cold the water is. Today will be the day.

I pull a pair of shorts and a gray hooded sweat-shirt over my bathing suit and slip out into the upstairs hall.

My father's snores rattle through the doorway of the big bedroom at the top of the stairs, and I pause outside before going down. The wooden steps groan softly under my feet, and the house seems to shift in its sleep. I creep through the living room, dining room, and kitchen and unlatch the screen door to the back porch. In the corner of the garage my fish-ing rod, tackle box, net, and bucket stand exactly where I left them last fall, which seems forever ago.

I run down the path to the lake, the pail banging against my bare leg. A scrim of blue mist drifts up from the water to join small clouds that hover low over the skyline. The birds twitter and chirp in the tall oak and maple trees that line the path to the dock.

I tie a silver spinner onto the leader at the end of my line. A great blue heron coasts across the water to land in the pickerelweed at the edge of the lake. The sun casts a golden glow over the hills on the opposite shoreline, and it's all reflected in the still, cold water.

I'd rather fish with bait, but since yesterday was the last day of school I haven't had time to hunt for worms or to look for the lone, pale crayfish that hides under the rowboat.

My first cast kerplunks into the lake, and there is a sharp jolt as a fish hits the lure. Rings spool out from flashes of yellow tail and bony lips, and my heart lifts sharply to see such light and heat in such cold water. The fish fights hard, diving and leaping as I reel him in. When I finally get him on the dock, his fins glow orange like the sunrise and his tail flicks icy water into my face as I unhook him. I fill the pail from the lake, put the fish in, and set it on the dock beside me. The fish lashes around for a minute and then lies still, his fins feathering the little water ferns beneath him.

The next two casts yield two more perch. But then the fish stop going for the lure. I watch the silver beads and little spoon swivel silently through the clear green water a couple of dozen times more before I set the rod aside and hang my bare legs over the edge of the dock.

I imagine myself spending most mornings this summer with my feet dangling off the dock, my dog stretched out beside me on the rough planks. He is black-and-tan, with long silky fur, a big pink tongue, and chocolate brown eyes. His name is Jeff. He rests his chin between his front paws and looks up at me, wagging his fluffy tail.

I don't actually have this dog yet, but I know exactly what he looks like and I've been thinking about how to get him.

I need a dog because I don't have any real friends. Occasionally my mother arranges for her friend Mrs. Mattise (also known as Aunt Dorothy) to bring her daughter, Carol, over to play with me. Carol is talented. She loves to sing and act, to perform for an audience. She doesn't like to fish.

Or my mother tells Mrs. Van Wert I'll stop by to play mumblety-peg with her son, Dale. Dale has cerebral palsy, and he can't go for walks in the woods. I like Dale, but I'm not crazy about playing mumblety-peg, which involves throwing a knife so its point sticks in the ground, and after a while I look for excuses to leave.

Sometimes Patty Moore comes when her mother visits my mother. She and Karen like to play with dolls, and I lose interest, although I love Patty.

"I don't want you to grow up without the gift of friendship," my mother says when I complain about her arranging for people to be my playmates. She and my father worry that I prefer to be alone. But the truth isn't so simple.

Karen and my older brother, Bobby, have friends from school who live near us. But none of my classmates live anywhere near where our house sits, on the south end of Chapman Lake in the wooded, rolling hills of northeastern Pennsylvania.

Secretly I long for a friend. When I was younger I invented a playmate, Judy, whom I adored. She was my constant companion. Judy was not tall and gawky like me. I have what Bobby calls bird legs, and I wear my stick-straight hair caught back at the sides in barrettes. Judy was petite and dimpled, with cascades of blond curls. She was sweet and cuddly, and like me she loved secrets. I told her everything.

I don't remember exactly when Judy abandoned me. It may have been the summer I turned seven and lost interest in dolls. It was the first year I was allowed to ride a bicycle on my own. It was the year

I discovered the mysteries of the woods and the depths of the lake and the beauty of the fish and birds. I don't think Judy shared my passions any more than Dale and Carol do.

I play a lot of pretend games as I fish and walk along trails through the primeval forest that begins at the edge of our garden. I daydream about having adventures in far-off places. I keep my ears tuned for exotic names. Srinagar. Shanghai. Istanbul. Casablanca. I love these words.

Last summer my grandmother Mema Fisher was visiting for a couple of weeks. One evening she sat on the sofa crocheting black squares with bright-colored centers. My little brother, Charlie, sat next to her, watching her fingers fly over the woolen yarn. The rest of us were scattered about the room. I had been reading.

"What's that?" I asked about the squares she'd sewn together that lay pooled in her lap.

"It's an afghan," Mema said, looking up from where the small table lamp beside her cast a circle of light on her work.

"Why's it called an afghan?" I knew what Mema would say as soon as the words were out of my mouth.

"Let's find out," she said, setting her crocheting aside. She led me upstairs, where a row of white-and-gold leather-bound volumes of the *Encyclopaedia Britannica* sat on one of the lower bookshelves at the end of the hallway.

She pulled out the volume marked "A," and together we looked up "afghan" and found it was a word that derived from Afghanistan, a mountainous tribal nation in Central Asia. For more than an hour we read, looking up things the Afghanistan entry cross-referenced in other volumes. Among other things, we learned that carrots and cauliflower—my two least favorite vegetables—were first cultivated there. It didn't say a word about the little woolen blanket my grandmother was crocheting.

But that entire summer, Afghanistan was the setting of many daydreams as I sat fishing on the dock. Even though I knew Afghanistan was landlocked, I always imagined arriving there by boat. I would be met by men in turbans and carried over the desert mountains in a chair balanced on a platform.

In the fall, when the *Buster Brown* show was on television, my adventures moved to India, where I rode high behind the head of an elephant, watching tigers creep through the jungle. And in February this

7

year, when we all went to a Chinese restaurant to celebrate my grandmother's birthday, my daydreams
moved to a vast land inhabited by people who wore
broad, pagoda-shaped hats and carried round
bamboo boxes filled with wonton, bird's nest soup,
and beggar's chicken home for the children's supper,
like the people in the pictures on the restaurant's
walls.

My mother associates my daydreaming with not
having friends, and both of these facts about me
worry her.

"Why don't you ask Billy McClosky to go fishing
with you?" she suggested last night when I told her I
was going out early this morning. My mother knows
Billy's mother, and she has decided he'd be a good
playmate for me. Billy McClosky has freckles, and
his ears stick out so far he reminds me of Charlie's
favorite teddy bear. He's nice enough, but at the end
of each summer his family moves back to the upper
reaches of New York State, where they live the rest of
the year.

"It's just easier to go fishing alone," I said. What I
didn't say was that I don't need Billy McClosky chat-
tering on the dock and scaring the fish away, not to
mention interrupting my exotic daydream adventures.

Or scuffling his feet along trails overlaid with dappled sunlight to let every living creature in the forest know we're coming. And I don't want to be indebted to anyone when it comes time to choose up sides for softball.

I am a bit of an odd duck—at least, that's what my grandmother says. But that doesn't mean I'm immune to loneliness. I don't need Billy McClosky for a friend. What I need is a dog.

I change my mind about the perch and empty the entire contents of the bucket back into the lake. I regret not having that liquid-silver taste of perch to look forward to for breakfast, but it's worth it to watch them dart off under the dock, so fast it's like magic—poof! They're gone. I gather up my rod and tackle and head back up to the house.

Yesterday, when my teacher handed over my report card, it was marked with straight A's. That perfect report card, which my mother proudly displayed on the buffet in the dining room for everyone to admire, fits perfectly into my plan to acquire what I want more than anything in the world: my dog, Jeff. The next step of the plan is to make breakfast for everyone.

I knew I could count on Karen, who has just finished third grade, to have a smattering of B's and C's on her report card. Karen is smart, but she hates school.

Bobby, who has just finished seventh grade, also brought home a less than stellar report card. He doesn't like school much, either. His real problem is that he's cursed with allergies. I'm tempted to say that I'm cursed with Bobby's allergies, because it always seems when I want something most the answer is no because of Bobby's tendency to itch and sneeze around anything that gives off dust, has fur, smells interesting—or involves a number of other impurities to which I'm attracted.

But that sounds really selfish, because Bobby suffers a lot, and I feel sorry for him. It's not just the sneezing and wheezing and coughing and itchy rashes. He's absent from school frequently because of being sick, and isn't able to make up everything by the end of the year. His mediocre grades aren't really his fault, and I feel a little guilty about taking advantage of having the best report card in the family. But I want my dog badly enough to do it anyway.

I put my fishing things back in the garage and slip into the kitchen. The house is still sleeping.

Being as quiet as I can be, I scramble eggs in a large skillet, toast most of a loaf of bread, pour six glasses of orange juice, and put coffee and water in the electric percolator. Everything is ready on the table by the time the members of my family straggle downstairs.

"I wanted my fish for breakfast," says Charlie, who is five. He grinds the backs of his fists into his eye sockets to chase away the last of sleep. Charlie has just graduated from using safety pins to real hooks on his fishing line. He keeps every single fish he's ever caught, no matter how small it is. He's become known as the "Minnow Murderer."

"What a nice surprise!" says my mother, who makes a big breakfast only on weekend mornings when my father has time to appreciate it. "I'll fix your fish for lunch," she says to Charlie.

"We-e-ell-ll! What's this?" booms my father in the exaggerated way he has of showing surprise. He's the biggest man in the world—at least, it seems so to me. He's six feet five inches tall, and wears size 14½ quadruple E shoes. He sits at the table and tucks a napkin into the neck of his shirt to cover his silk tie. He eats his eggs and toast quickly, gulps down his juice and coffee, and kisses us all goodbye with loud lip smacks before heading off for work in the city of Scranton, about twelve miles away.

After breakfast I begin to clear the table and offer to do the dishes myself. My mother looks up from packing snacks for Charlie and glances at me. I hate washing dishes and don't usually volunteer to do them. But it's part of my plan for acquiring this dog.

Mom is taking Charlie with her to do the grocery shopping in Jermyn, which is five miles away. Charlie stands beside her, watching her spread peanut butter on graham crackers, his close-clipped blond hair shining like a golden helmet in the sunlight that pours through the kitchen window. His face is peppered with freckles. He has an infectious grin and guileless green eyes, but he has an alarming knack for getting into trouble whenever he's more than a few feet away from our mother.

"Will Daddy be home for dinner tonight?" I ask. (I ask casually, but it's a detail of strategic importance to my plan.) Mom packs about a dozen crackers in waxed-paper bags. Charlie watches her every move. He is always hungry. One time he told some men working on the electrical lines along Brown Hollow Road that he was a starving orphan with nobody to feed him. He tried to beg cigarettes from them—he said he was sixteen but he'd shrunk from smoking. They ended up giving him sizable pieces of their sandwiches.

"As far as I know, Daddy will be home around five," my mother says, loading everything into a cooler. Although she'll only be gone for two hours, she has to pack enough food for two days, because Charlie gets frantic when he's hungry. Before she leaves, she asks Karen and me to clean the bathrooms and bedrooms.

Karen rests her reddish curly head on one folded arm, pushing her eggs around on her plate with her fork. I know Karen hates eggs that aren't cooked until they're as hard as rubber, but it's not Karen I'm trying to impress with breakfast. Again I feel guilty. Karen has beautiful sunny-sky-colored eyes, which are never completely open before 10 a.m.

"Did you hear me?" my mother asks.

"Yup!" I say cheerfully. (I love mornings.) Karen glares at me.

"Karen?" Mom asks, cocking an eyebrow at my sister, who is still mostly asleep. "Karen!"

My sister scowls and says, "Yes." Mom sighs and says goodbye. She loads Charlie and enough toys to last a week into the car. Charlie also tends to get bored easily, and that's when he gets into trouble. Bobby goes out to the garage to scrape the old paint from the hull of the canoe in preparation for repainting.

Bobby is possessed by the idea of owning and driving an automobile. The canoe is just a stand-in until he's old enough to have his own car, which is still four years away.

Karen is only a year and a half younger than I am, but we don't hang around together much. She and her friends like to paint their nails. Then they pretend they're wives cooking dinner for their husbands, holding the tips of their fingers up in the air so they don't get messed up. For the life of me I don't understand why anyone would make their hands useless by putting nail polish on them. Other times they pretend they're mothers whose kids won't clean up their rooms, or nurses tending hospital patients. All of these things are impossible to do with painted nails.

I don't want to paint my nails or wear grownup clothes or drive a car. I want to be able to explore the woods and play softball and paddle a canoe. I don't want my own house—I want to stay with my family forever. I know there really is no such thing as forever, but I like to pretend there is.

Karen and I make a deal that I will vacuum and dust the bedrooms and she will clean the bathrooms. Technically, my part is more work, but I can do it really quickly when I have things to do afterward, so I don't mind. After I finish my chores and put the vacuum cleaner away, I leave Karen still scrubbing toilet bowls and head out the back door, through the yard, and down the path to the forest that comes right up to the edge of our property.

I read somewhere that the Lenape Indians who lived in these forests of the Pocono Mountains walked silently by stepping first on the balls of their feet, which are more sensitive than the heels. I've been practicing walking that way so that the deer and pheasants and rabbits and raccoons and foxes and beavers can't hear me coming. I can feel twigs and sticks and dried leaves before they have a chance to snap and rustle underfoot. I'm getting to be pretty silent in my genuine deerskin moccasins.

I search for animals to bring home. I keep small tanks and large glass bowls sitting on the screened front porch. Each summer they contain a rotating collection of crayfish, turtles, grasshoppers, crickets, an occasional snake, toads, minnows, salamanders, frogs, praying mantises, butterflies, moths, and caterpillars.

I keep them for a few days and then turn them back to the woods. This is something I can't imagine Carol Mattise or Karen or Bobby or Billy McClosky doing, because it takes such a delicate way of walking to catch these creatures.

In the garage is a wire cage with a bed of toweling in one corner that's reserved for the injured— once it was a chipmunk whose tail had been snapped off by a neighborhood cat. Another time it was a dazed bird that had sailed into our dining room window and broken its wing.

I reach the creek (which we pronounce "crick") that bounces in silvery riffles over rocks and fallen tree limbs down to the lake. I turn upstream toward the pond, where a week ago I found frog's eggs. They looked like a black-speckled mass of jelly suspended among the stalks of cattails in a shallow area along the shore of the pond. I went back every day after school to watch them develop. When I returned to the pond the day before the last day of school, they hadn't hatched yet.

Now I find several tadpoles swimming among the stalks in the shallow water. They look like tiny black minnows. When my shadow falls on them, they flick their tails and make little *plips* in the water.

As I watch, several more wriggle out of their egg casings. They shake until they're free of the jelly mass that holds the eggs, and continue to wiggle joyously as they swim into the sunlight.

I think I know how those tadpoles feel, because I feel pretty much the same way the first day after the last day of school, filled with the prospect of an endless summer of golden days with my new dog.

DOGLESS DAYS

I am so absorbed in the tadpoles I don't notice at first that their piece of the pond has separated from the rest of the water. The water is brilliant with clouds of green algae that look like they'd suffocate a baby tadpole. It's been an unusually cold but dry spring, and their little pool of water looks barely half the size it was when I was here a couple of days ago. One more day and they might be beached.

I remember seeing an old coffee can alongside the trail and retrace my steps until I spot its rusty rim half-buried in dead leaves. I race back to the drying pool and scoop up the tadpoles, being careful not to squish any with the edges of the can. I think I got them all, as well as the jelly mass of still-unhatched eggs. They should survive in one of the tanks on the porch until rain comes to refill the pond.

The water leaks slowly from the rusty coffee can, so I carry the tadpoles home carefully, making my steps tiny and quick so I don't slosh them and the pond water onto the ground. There is not a cloud of any description in the brilliant turquoise sky that sits like a bowl inverted over the woods and pond.

About halfway home, it occurs to me that all of the tanks and bowls on the front porch are full. I go over the contents of each in my mind to decide which to empty to make a home for this family of aspiring frogs. The baby snapping turtles are still pretty small to feed themselves. If I let the Japanese beetle grubs go, I'll miss the hatch and they'll eat my mother's roses. I really have grown attached to the minnows. And I hope it's only a matter of days until the pale gray chrysalis turns into a blue-and-black butterfly.

I decide to release a one-clawed crayfish I rescued last week from a fight with the crayfish that lives under our rowboat. The tadpoles are far more interesting than the crayfish, which I think probably could survive with only one claw.

I go straight to the bathroom near the kitchen and dump the tadpoles into the toilet bowl to keep them safe until I empty out the crayfish and fill its tank with pond water, mud, and vegetation.

Nobody is home, except for Bobby, who is out in the garage, still scraping paint from the canoe and sanding the teak gunwales.

I love having a purpose like saving animals. The time flies when I'm doing something important. I think about the dog I'm going to get, and I don't mind so much being alone. He'll have a sixth sense for finding tadpoles, and we'll collect them together every June. I imagine harnessing tanks to his back— like baskets carried by the donkeys in photographs Uncle Paul brought back from Mexico—so we can collect animals all day in the woods.

I cradle the crayfish bowl in my arms and walk down to the lake. I wish him luck as I tip him into the water and watch him scoot backwards until he finds a large flat rock to take refuge under. Then I race back to the pond and refill the bowl for the tadpoles.

I carefully scoop up handfuls of black pond-bed muck and layer it on the bottom of the bowl, then add a few pieces of weed and fill the bowl to the top with green, scummy pond water so the tadpoles will have plenty to eat. I hold the bowl up to the sunlight to watch the swirling particles of mud settle. Little animals with curled bodies the size of dust specks dart back and forth. I rush home, snatch up my bait net from the back porch, and head straight to the bathroom.

When I get there, the toilet bowl is empty—the tadpoles are gone! My mother's car is parked in the driveway, but she isn't in the house. I run in a panic out to the garage, but the canoe sits alone, its half-scraped hull pointing toward the ceiling. The over-head light has been turned off and Bobby isn't there. I stand still for a moment, trying to calm my thundering heart. Surely I am mistaken. I go back and tap the side of the toilet bowl with the metal handle of my net to see if perhaps they've just moved out of the open water of the bowl to take refuge in the more confined water of the pipe. But that toilet bowl is just plain empty.

I imagine my tadpoles making their perilous journey through the sewage system, where they will die a horrible death of asphyxiation. It's a disgusting way to die—and they're only babies!

I run down to the beach, still clutching my bait net in one hand. In the first warm days of June, everyone spends every possible moment lying beside the water in the sun to make up for the months the lake was locked in ice and they were locked indoors. Beach chairs and towels dot the grass and sand like a patchwork quilt.

"Mom!" I shout, not seeing her at first. "Someone flushed the toilet!" Surprised stares aim in my direction, and a few snickers emanate from the wood-and-canvas beach chairs where I spot my mother sitting with two of her friends who live around the bend in the lakeshore. She looks up at me, shading her eyes with her arm.

"Come over here and tell me what the problem is," she says. No doubt my blurting out the astonishing news that someone has flushed the toilet embarrasses her.

I try to explain what happened, but tears sting the backs of my eyes and my throat closes as I think of my baby frogs slowly dying in septic sludge. Now that I've got everybody's attention, I can't hold back the tears. Bobby comes dripping up from the dock and flops his sodden body onto his beach towel.

"What's the matter?" he asks. My mother holds me by the arm and turns her head to explain the problem to him.

"Did you see her tadpoles?" she asks.

"Well," he says, looking uncertain, "I did use the

downstairs toilet. And, yes, I flushed it. You always tell me to flush it. But I didn't see any tadpoles. Who keeps tadpoles in the toilet, anyway?"

"He did it on purpose!" I wail, not really believing that he did.

"Don't be silly," my mother says. Behind her shoulder, Bobby's face looks guilty and embarrassed. "Tell your sister you're sorry," she says, turning toward him again.

My mother leans forward to wipe the tears from my face with the flat of her hand.

"Sorry," Bobby says, ducking his head and flopping back onto his towel.

"Why don't you go for a swim?" she asks me. "The water is beautiful, and they've put the float in." I already know that because I was the first one down to the lake this morning. But I don't say it. I sniffle loudly, trying to get my tears under control. I shake my head. "Well, then go find something to feed to the turtles," she suggests. The two baby snapping turtles on the front porch don't like domestic turtle food.

"Okay," I say with one last, loud snuffle.

"Sorry," Bobby repeats, so softly I barely hear him. But I can't answer because I'm afraid I'll cry again. I turn away and my mother calls me back to accept his apology. I put my head down and race off toward the creek.

I'm not too excited about doing much of anything for the rest of the day. In addition to feeling terrible about the tadpoles, I'm impatient for my father to come home. I plan to ask at dinner whether I can have a dog, but waiting is hard.

I flip my net around halfheartedly, trying to snag some insects for the turtles. I catch about a dozen gnats, but it's a cool, sunny, breezy day—not a good day for catching mosquitoes, which is what the turtles like best. I do find two perfect halves of a robin's egg, the palest blue, and still wet inside. I look around for the nest, but I don't see it.

Dragonflies shimmer over the edge of the creek, but they're too big for the turtles to eat, so I sit on a flat rock beside a little pool and watch them hover like luminescent green, blue, and silver helicopters over the softly gurgling water.

At home I find some good dried houseflies on the upstairs windowsills, and my mother's compost bin yields some edible morsels: carrot shavings, celery root, apple peels, and some wilted outer lettuce leaves. From the bread box I filch the heels from a

24

loaf of bread my mother has brought from the market. I sort through what I've collected and portion it out to the animals in the bowls and tanks. They always act as if they don't notice I've fed them, but when I come back the food is either gone or partly eaten.

Later in the afternoon, whitecaps foam on the lake against the bruised, low-hung sky. My mother dashes up from the beach, the canvas of the beach chairs flapping from one hand and the other holding on to Charlie's wrist. The wind plasters the skirt of her swimming suit against her thighs and blows her short, wavy hair back against her head as if it's wet. Karen comes scurrying across the road from Harriet McAndrews' house, her beach towel flying out behind her like Superman's cape.

I go up to our room to find my favorite book—*Black Beauty*—which I'm reading for the third time. I sit on the glider on the screened front porch, beneath the wide sill that holds the bowls and tanks containing my animals, to wait for my father. The rain beats on the roof overhead, and when the wind turns, a fine mist sifts through the screen, leaving my skin damp and cool. Rags of lightning crack and pop in the sky.

My mind keeps drifting from the book, and before I know it, my dog is sitting beside me, cocking his floppy ears as the thunder rolls. Soon I fall asleep, and I dream of him sleeping next to me on the big brass bed. I dream happily until my mother wakes me to set the table for dinner.

I'm clumsy with the silverware, dropping everything before I get it to the table, knocking over the salt, and spilling water on the tablecloth. I'm very nervous about asking if I can have a dog.

"Dad's home," Bobby shouts. He wants Dad to take him to Sugerman's to get a new softball for the next day's game—the first of the season. Charlie always gets noisy when our father comes home. Everyone has something they want to ask him or tell him. I'm glad, because nobody notices my clumsiness. We have ham and coleslaw and baked beans for dinner, which I like. But I can't eat.

"Don't play with your food," my mother says. My father looks over at me—I sit just to the left of his place at the head of the table. I sit up straight and purposefully spear a piece of ham with my fork.

"Can I have a dog?" I blurt out. I'd meant to ask more casually. "I got all A's on my report card!"

"Yeah!" says Karen. "A puppy!"

"You know Bobby's allergic to dogs," my mother says, cutting up another slice of ham for Charlie. "Say 'yes,' not 'yeah,'" she says to Karen.

"Oh, please?" I say, feeling as if I might break into tears again. This is *not* going as I'd hoped it would. "I'll keep him in my room." Karen nods her head up and down—she likes dogs, too. "I'll feed him outside. I'll take care of him. He'll go everywhere with me!"

"No," my mother says, folding her napkin by the side of her plate. "You know we can't have animals with fur. And you already have dozens with scales and shells and slithery skin. Why don't you make friends with some of the kids you took swimming lessons with last year? I'm sure you could find someone who'd like to fish with you."

"Nobody likes to do the kind of stuff I like," I say. "That's why I need a dog." I flop against the back of my chair, which groans behind my weight, and fold my arms across my chest.

"Your mother said no," my father says. When he speaks in that tone of voice, he's warning us not to argue. I sit through the rest of dinner in silence, bitterly disappointed. I don't touch my dessert, which is tapioca, or fish eyes, according to Bobby. I don't even eat the whipped cream or the maraschino cherry on top, which I usually eat first.

I thought for sure they'd say yes. I will *never* have a dog, and suddenly I feel exposed and lost—like the orphan Charlie likes to claim to be.

It's my turn to dry the dishes, with Karen washing. We clear the table in silence. I try hard not to spill anything, and when I drop two slices of ham from the platter my mother doesn't say anything, but she swishes a washcloth in the soapy water and wrings it out to wipe up the linoleum. If we had a dog he could clean it up. I don't say it.

In the living room my father sits in his chair with his feet stretched out on his ottoman, catching up on the newspapers he hasn't had time to read all week. My father has his own business selling X-ray machines to clinics and hospitals. He's away a lot— on the road, he calls it—and he likes his rare quiet evenings at home. My mother sits across the living room from him reading a book. I lean on the arm of her chair. She ignores me for a while, then looks up at me with one raised eyebrow.

"Can I go out—"

"May I—" my mother says.

"May I go out and catch some worms so I can go fishing tomorrow?"

"Wear a slicker. And stay in our yard," she says.

I pull on my yellow rain slicker. I don't wear the hood, because the rain has almost stopped. It's essential not to wear shoes so you can feel the night crawlers with your toes. The grass is cold and the soles of my feet tingle. I've developed a sure method of catching the fat worms that fish—particularly bass, perch, and sunfish—love to eat, especially early in the morning when I like to fish. In one hand I carry a bucket filled with damp dirt, and in the other I carry a heavy flashlight. It's unusually dark for nine o'clock because the sky has been crowded with dense clouds since afternoon.

The white circle of light shines on the deep red tip of a beauty that protrudes nearly two inches from the gray clay soil. In one motion I drop the bucket and flashlight and pounce forward onto the night crawler. The next part is a delicate, life-or-death tug-of-war. I hold on tightly enough so that the worm cannot pull back into the earth, but not so tightly that he'll snap into pieces. I've watched robins do this. They just hold on until the worm relaxes, and then they give a tug, exposing another half inch at a time. It works.

Worm hunting would be more efficient with a friend—someone to carry the bucket and hold the flashlight so I can see where I'm pouncing. I just don't know anyone who has that kind of patience. My sister can't even stand to look at worms.

In very little time I have a dozen fat night crawlers, enough for a few days of fishing, and all that will stay alive in the bucket.

The curtains hang still in the living room window, giving no sign that anyone is about to call me into the house for bed. I switch off the flashlight, set the bucket beside the back steps, and run down to the lake. The reflected light from the windows winks like starlight on the wet grass.

I sit on the rough planks and swing my cold, wet feet out over the edge of the dock. I shine the flashlight into the water, half-hoping to catch a glimpse of the legendary man-sized fish that populate the murky depths of Chapman Lake and half-afraid I might actually see one. Chapman Lake is a glacial lake, carved out by the creeping of an ice mass millions of years before.

Once, a long time ago, a boy whose family owned property not far from ours on the spring-fed lake took a leaking canoe out after school one October day. The canoe quickly filled with water and sank into the autumn-chilled lake. The boy became entangled in weeds, and drowned. Divers from Scott Township Dive and Rescue spent several days in scuba gear looking for his body. Until then nobody seemed to realize that Chapman Lake was several hundred feet deep in places. Its bed is granite pocked with deep, dark caves. In their powerful underwater searchlights the rescuers saw bizarre-looking fish with narrow bodies six and seven feet long and eyes that were blind for lack of light. The fish, it was told for years after, were thought to be extinct everywhere else in the world.

By the time the body was found, wrapped in lake grasses and trapped under a rock ledge deep below the surface, Chapman Lake had become a local legend because of its bizarre and ancient fish. I shiver and pull back my legs, scramble to my feet, and run all the way back to the house.

While Karen is brushing her teeth, my mother comes into the bedroom to say good night.

"Would you do me a favor?" she asks, sitting on the edge of my bed. I nod sleepily. "When you find yourself thinking about wanting a dog, will you think instead of finding a friend?" I start to protest, but she holds up her hand to silence me. "I know you're lonely," she goes on. "You need someone to do things with. It can be more than one person. One day you could go swimming with Patty. Another day you could fish with Billy. You need to control your imagination. And you need to learn to go along with what other people want to do."

"But if I start thinking about a dog, how do I stop?" I ask. "It just comes into my head."

"Think about something else," she says. "Like changing the subject." I ponder this for a minute.

"Just now I tried to change the subject. I tried to think of someone who knew how to catch night crawlers. I can't think of a single person who understands about being quiet enough not to scare them back into the ground. I don't need a friend—I need a dog!"

DOG IN DANGER

The next morning is Saturday. Under a deep blue sky still sprinkled with morning stars, I head down to the dock with my fishing pole, tackle box, and the bucket of worms. In the first hour I catch six sunfish, their broad, flat sides gleaming blue and green, their stomachs the color of egg yolks.

I cast my line from a rickety disused dock that sticks out from a weedy stretch of shore. I think about what my mother said last night. Every time I catch myself about to fall into a daydream about my dog Jeff, I try to change the subject.

I think about the season's first softball game, which will be this very evening, right after dinner. I've been looking forward to it since the last game on Labor Day last year. I imagine the prickle of the day's sunburn on my shoulders, the deepening shadows as the sun sets, the crack of the wooden bat, and the gleam of the softball as it rises against the darkening sky. My teammates' cheers ring in the air as I catch the player out at first base.

As I ponder this, I can't help noticing the mist rise from the mirror-calm surface of the lake. Reflected there before me are mounds of puffy clouds. One of them takes the shape of a large round head with flopping ears—it's Jeff! The dog's body forms in the clouds. Jeff, with his silky ears and bright eyes, will walk the woods beside me and show me where animals I'd never have seen otherwise lie hidden in the hollows of old trees.

Trying not to daydream about a dog is useless, and I think sadly about what an undisciplined mind I have.

I catch several perch too small to keep, plus two good-sized ones. At about nine, when the sun begins to burn my shoulders, I carry the eight gill-strung fish up to scale and clean on a wooden table in the backyard. I continue my dog daydream as I work. Jeff's bark is deep and serious, not yappy and whining like Dale Van Wert's dog, Cindy.

I fry one perch in sizzling butter for breakfast and

wrap the other seven fish in waxed paper and stow them in the freezer. I like to save fish until there are enough for the whole family for dinner. When Jeff comes to live with me, I'll slip him pieces of fish to eat under the table. He likes fish as much as I do.

After breakfast I go into the dining room, where my mother works at her sewing machine making skirts for Karen and me for school next fall. I don't even want to think about school. A piece of navy-and-forest-green plaid wool is spread out around her. A dozen straight pins protrude from between my mother's clamped lips as the machine whirs away.

"Mom," I begin, and realize my voice sounds a little whiny. I clear my throat and start again. "If we keep a dog out in the garage, or in the basement, Bobby . . ." She stops the machine and slides her eyes over at me, carefully extracting the pins from her mouth.

"I said no last night. Don't ask me again just because your father isn't here." My father and Bobby have gone out to buy a new softball and catcher's mitt. The pins clatter lightly as she drops them into a turquoise blue saucer on the table beside her. I want to argue with her but she gives me a warning glance. I go away disappointed.

I understand why she's afraid of Bobby getting sick again. He has spent several of his first twelve Christmases and birthdays in an oxygen tent in Mercy Hospital in Scranton. Karen and I have grown so used to the ambulance coming in the middle of the night to take him away that we sometimes sleep right through it. What I don't understand is why my mother can't see how much I need a dog.

Our first softball game saves me from despair. That afternoon I help my father and Bobby cut the weeds in the field on the corner just across the street from our house. We gather to play right after dinner, and the sweet smell of wild grass still lingers in the air as Bobby and his best friend, Dougie Truman, choose teams. I am the second person Dougie chooses, which makes my heart do a little jig in my chest. My brother never chooses me, and I can run faster than he can. He can hit and throw the ball harder, but I can catch better.

I play first base because I'm not afraid of a ball thrown hard or of getting run over by the runner. I love the smell of the grass cooling and the dust settling, and my first time at bat I hit the ball hard and it sails out over the head of Tommy Stafford, the center fielder on Bobby's team. I drive Dougie in to score from second base, and make it to second myself.

The thing I love most about softball is the way the team works together, encouraging each other and pushing ourselves to run faster, throw harder, keep our eyes on the ball, to be more than we are as individuals. I love everything about softball except losing. And tonight we beat Bobby's team nine to seven. Sweet victory.

I don't think once about my dog until it grows too dark to see. My father crosses the street to get a flashlight from our house so he and Bobby can walk Dougie home. I sit on the front porch steps waiting for them to come back. I'm too excited to go to bed and want to talk about the game. My mother and Karen and Charlie are walking Patty home, and I'm alone. Early stars begin to pop out while the sky is still a dark blue, and I contemplate how far away they are, that they are fiery bodies like the sun, which we talked about in science class. I wonder whether there is life out there, on other places more like the earth. I will not daydream.

At first I don't have trouble keeping my mind on track because contemplating outer space and the stars is pretty interesting. But then without my even noticing, a little daydream takes over. It goes like this: I hit the ball with a huge *thwack*—so hard it hangs high in the air among the early stars for what seems minutes before flying out of the field, across the road, and into the knee-deep grass that covers the field on the other side. It's almost dark—just as it is in real time—and my dog Jeff, who has been watching obediently from beyond the first-base line, races out into the vacant field and finds the ball. The outfielders chase after him, waving their arms and shouting for him to drop the ball, which he does just as I cross home plate.

The following days seem endless, shimmering with sunlight and filled with swimming and fishing and adventures in the woods. I spend a lot of time daydreaming about my dog as I fish. I come home at the end of long afternoons knowing somehow I will have a dog of my own.

And then something truly miraculous happens.

My father announces that he has bought a building in Scranton. His business has expanded quickly from selling X-ray machines to fixing them when they're broken, cleaning them regularly, and supplying

X-ray chemicals and film. The company has rented part of a building from another business, but it has run out of room.

"This building is big enough to grow into!" my father says, gesturing extravagantly with his enormous hands. His excitement about his new building is contagious. I'm excited. We're all excited.

The next day is Saturday, and the entire family piles into our blue sedan and drives twelve miles into Scranton to inspect the new building, soon to be the new headquarters of my father's X-ray business.

It's a hot summer day, and the air seems to shimmer above the surface of Route 6. About halfway between our house and the city we see something large lumbering along beside the median strip of the four-lane highway ahead of us. As we get closer, we see clearly a large tan-and-black dog with a rope attached to his collar. He appears to be looking for something or someone, turning to peek over his shoulder and swiveling his head this way and that.

My heart beats in the middle of my throat when I see the danger he's in, with cars whizzing past in the two lanes beside him, some swerving and missing him by only inches. My father slows in the passing lane to avoid hitting him as we approach, and just then the dog sits beside the median strip, as if giving up his search.

"Can we take him home?" I ask. There is no answer from the front seat. The dog has silky black fur, with tan feathers on his haunches and tail. Suddenly I realize this is the dog I'd been dreaming of! This is Jeff!

"Stop the car, Bob," my mother says.

"Why stop?" my father asks. "He's got a rope tied to his collar. He belongs to someone." Our car moves at barely a crawl. Horns blare as cars slow down in both lanes behind us.

"What would he be doing out here on the highway?" my mother asks. The dog's tongue lolls wet and pink from the side of his mouth and he looks up. His eyes are bright and intelligent, a golden liquid brown. He half rises from his haunches and rolls his ears forward. Unsure of whether the dog might get up and run toward us, my father does as my mother asks, and stops the car.

The dog scans the three faces—Bobby's, Karen's, and mine—crowded at the rear window on the driver's side of the car.

"Keep your hands inside," my mother warns. "You don't know if he'll bite or if he's sick." The dog's ears pitch back and forward again as if he hears her, and he pulls his tongue into his mouth, suddenly looking less tired and more alert. He continues to stare at the three of us in the back window. My father lets the car roll forward a bit and the dog rises to his feet again, as if to follow. It's all I can do to keep from bolting from the car and dragging him to safety.

"Mom!" I say, knowing full well that she also loves dogs. "We should save him. This traffic is going fifty miles an hour. He'll be hit by a car or a truck! I'll take care of him. Please, Mom?"

"Please!" Karen says. "We want a dog." Charlie bounces up and down on the seat between my parents and makes a sound something like a dog's bark.

"He belongs to someone," my father says, putting his foot on the accelerator.

"No!" I shout. "This isn't just any dog. This is the dog I've been dreaming of. Please, Dad! He'll be killed!" I'm in a panic. But the car begins to gather speed.

"In a few minutes he'll be squished flat on the road," I say. "Mom! Do something!"

"Your father said no," my mother says in a tight little voice without turning her head. "Besides, your brother's allergies—"

"He could sleep in the garage," Bobby says. He likes dogs, too, even though they send him into fits of coughing and sneezing and leave him scratching at bright red rashes on his inner arms. "If he isn't in the house, he won't make me sick."

I still think my father will stop, but instead he steps harder on the accelerator and the car hurtles down the highway. I get up on my knees and look out the rear window at the large tan-and-black dog with the rope tied to his collar, the perfect dog—who by then is a tiny speck, a sitting duck in the middle of the passing lane.

"How could you leave him out here to die in the road?" I shout at my father. I am stunned.

The silence in the front seat is stony. I sense that my mother doesn't approve of my father's not stopping, but she won't do anything about it. Having wheedled and begged, I can do nothing now but feel miserable, and this I do, pain burning in the pit of my stomach and in my heart.

The rest of the drive I sit wedged into my corner of the backseat, arms clasped tightly around my middle, trying to keep myself from flying apart with grief for Jeff—the dog I've been dreaming of.

Charlie kneels on the front seat and looks over

the back of it at me. "Mom," he says, "Suzanne's crying."

"I am not!" I say, my voice crumbling and tears rolling down my face. I turn toward the window, and my mother pulls Charlie to sit facing forward again. I try desperately to keep from thinking. But images and sounds hurl themselves at me—the screech of tires and the dull thud of impact, Jeff flying through the air and landing with a heavy *thwack* on the cinder shoulder of the road.

Nobody talks the rest of the way to Mulberry Street, where my father's building sits at the end of a driveway that runs between a dry cleaner's and a pharmacy to a large, dust-blown lot that extends from behind the pharmacy to the river.

"Will you be able to get trucks in and out of here?" my mother asks. Her voice sounds hollow and false. My father talks about widening the driveway as we get out of the car and walk toward the white stucco building.

Paper litters the floors of the warehouse and offices, and the windows are dusty. I walk apart from everyone else.

Bobby is impressed by the size of the new building. He runs from cavernous room to cavernous room, stopping to tilt back his head and shout, "Hellow-ow, hello-o-ow-ow!," his mouth aimed toward the ceiling.

At the driveway end of the building is a large concrete cargo dock where delivery trucks will back up to unload heavy equipment to be lifted by a small crane and dropped gently onto pallets that will be carried inside on the open arms of a forklift.

I go outside and sit on the bank overlooking the river, tossing small rocks down toward the water.

"Suzanne!" yells my mother. "Come away from there. Quit moping." She's in a bad mood, and I think she might be mad at my father.

After a while we go to Preno's, a fine Italian restaurant in Scranton, to celebrate with a spaghetti dinner. Usually spaghetti is my favorite thing to eat.

My father orders spaghetti with meatballs, salad, and garlic bread for everyone. He and my mother each have a glass of red wine. My father proposes a toast.

"To Reliance Medical X-Ray Company, Inc.!" he says, tilting his glass toward my mother's. We children raise our milk glasses. I sit holding the milk in my mouth, trying to swallow. Images of Jeff ducking trucks as big as the ones that will carry my father's

X-ray machines flash unbidden through my consciousness. I imagine Jeff lying on his side, his feet out in front of him at the edge of the road, a trickle of blood all that's left of the life that was in him. I see his expressive brown eyes that had looked up at us so hopefully as the car passed, now lifeless and staring. I wish I could control my imagination.

A SMALL MIRACLE

We get home very late. The fireflies wink their beacons under the crab apple tree in the side yard as we straggle sleepily up the front walk. I am the first one to the front porch steps, so I see him first.

There, sitting on the landing, curled up on the hemp mat in front of the screen door, is the big tan-and-black dog with the rope still attached to his collar. He's sound asleep, but when he hears us he opens an eye, lifts his tail, and lets it fall with a loud thump. I think I'm dreaming until I hear my mother behind me.

She's carrying Charlie, who is sleeping in her arms. At first she doesn't say anything, just sucks in her breath.

"Bob!" she says, her voice soft with disbelief. "Come here—you won't believe this!" And he doesn't, really, not at first. My father looks at my mother as if to ask what kind of joke we're playing on him.

"What . . . How?" he stammers. My father is never at a loss for words, and suddenly we kids are wide awake and talking, our voices stumbling over and bumping into each other.

"We have to keep him!" I say. "He risked his life to find us." There's no question in my mind. "Dad! This is the exact dog I've been dreaming about! This is *the dog*!"

"Please, Dad?" Karen asks.

"This was meant to be!" says Bobby, who tends to think that way.

"He was at least six miles away when we saw him this afternoon," my mother says, her voice still filled with wonder. My father can only nod. Did this dog wander so far in our direction by coincidence? Or perhaps someone saw us stop and traced our license plate number to deliver Jeff to our doorstep. We will never know what turn of fortune has brought Jeff to us. But there's no doubt that we are his new family. He is finally home.

I bend to him with my hand out. He seems

47

barely able to lift his head, but he stretches out that enormous pink tongue and licks my fingers. His tail thumps again.

"His name is Jeff," I announce. Nobody seems to have any problem with his name.

My mother hustles Bobby inside and tells me to take Jeff to the basement. Bobby looks back over his shoulder as my mother herds him through the screen door. I pick up the other end of the rope that's still attached to his collar, but it isn't necessary.

"Come on, Jeff!" I say, trying to act as if his being there is the most natural thing that could be. I'm giddy with the thought of the coincidence that brought him to me. It's as if I've been expecting him for a long time—I'm not even surprised. Jeff rises wearily to his feet, stretches, and limps behind me, around to the back of the house, through the garage, and down into the basement. I flick on the light and find some old beach towels that I fold carefully to make a bed for him on the landing of the basement staircase. I sit for a few minutes stroking his silky ears. Jeff closes his eyes and sighs.

The next morning I'm up long before daylight. I fix some scrambled eggs, spoon cottage cheese over them, tear up some bread, and mix it all together in a large bowl. Jeff eats it hungrily in the backyard, then licks my face.

The pads of his feet are nearly worn off, and his toenails are ground down to bloody little stubs. My mother finds salve for me to put on them, and I sit with him most of the day in the shade of the backyard, taking him for short walks at the edge of the woods. I want to watch him, get to know him. In fact, I stare at him for hours, unable to believe he's really my dog. My father still hasn't said yes, you can keep him. But he also hasn't said no. I have many plans for things Jeff and I will do together, but this first day I'm happy to let him rest.

The second day Jeff seems full of life and up for an adventure. His limp is gone, and he no longer walks in that dog-tired way with his head down and his ears drooping. We buy dog food at the feed store, and he eats every morsel of kibble we put out for him, and drinks two whole bowls of water.

Karen and I lie on our stomachs on the grass in the yard, watching the way his tongue curls backward in the bowl, scooping up water like a misdirected spoon. Everything about him fascinates and delights us. Karen wanders off to look for Patty, and I spend the rest of a second afternoon watching my dog.

The following day I take him fishing. He sits on the dock, his paws curled over the edge, quiet but watchful. I think he must have been someone's fishing dog, if there is such a thing. He never moves a muscle until the line goes taut, and then he jumps to his feet and leans way forward, with his nose nearly touching the water. His forehead is all puckered up, but he remains silent until the fish lands on the dock, and then he leaps about, barking and carrying on like a true fisherman!

During quiet moments I sit stroking his ears with one hand, the other holding my fishing rod. I think fiercely that I will never let this end. Not ever, ever, ever.

When we get home, I realize I haven't had one daydream the entire morning. I'm cured, I think. It seems like another miracle.

After a few days Karen complains that I'm hogging the dog.

"He's not just your dog," she says.

"He is!" I say with more feeling than necessary. "I take care of him. I'm the one who wanted a dog!"

"He belongs to the entire family," my mother says at dinner that night.

"I take care of him," I say again.

"You always get up so early that nobody else can feed him and take him for a walk," Karen says.

"You're getting too wrapped up in that dog," my mother says to me. "You're going to have to take turns." I agree grudgingly that the next day Karen can feed Jeff in the morning and play with him during the day.

"You have to get up early," I say. "He's always up and awake when I come down to feed him." Karen just looks at me. "Do you want me to feed him in the morning? You can play with him whenever you want all day long and feed him at night." Karen shrugs. I know she doesn't want to get up as early as I do—she might not even be physically able to get up that early.

I am up before six the next morning and I feed Jeff, then take him for a run at the edge of the woods. He loves running through the dew-wet grass, nose to the ground. He stops every once in a while and sneezes, then flips over onto his back and kicks his legs into the air. I imagine this is an expression of doggy joy. Karen stays in bed until nearly nine.

"Today you're going to have to play girl games," I explain to Jeff as I put him back in the basement. "Tomorrow you and I are going to roam the woods looking for animals to bring home!" I hold his muzzle lightly between my hands and Jeff looks me straight in the eye as I talk, then plants his pink, wet tongue on my cheek. The thought of having a quiet companion in the woods, one who loves being there as much as I do, fills me with a powerful, sweet longing.

After Karen has eaten her breakfast, she comes to the basement, where I still sit with Jeff.

"Didn't you go fishing?" she asks. I shake my head no. I'm going out to the woods and I wish Jeff could come with me.

"See you later," I say, scratching his ears.

"Bye," says Karen.

I haven't been long in the woods when I decide to see what Karen and Jeff are up to. It takes me a while to find them. I spot Karen having difficulty pushing the big old baby carriage our mother used to take us around in when we were little. It's been in the basement for the last three and a half years, ever since Charlie fell out on his head and refused to ride in it anymore.

The carriage looks heavy, and rocks from side to side, making Karen's progress along the edge of the road slow and tentative. Must be a huge baby, I think. Karen often baby-sits for families with little kids, but I don't know of any families in the neighborhood with babies small enough to ride in the carriage.

"Where's Jeff?" I ask, hoping she's grown tired of hanging out with him and put him back in the basement. Karen turns and gives me an odd look. She doesn't answer. "Whose baby is in there?" I ask, bending forward to see under the pop-up hood.

Jeff's wet black nose and bright eyes peer out at me from under a lace-edged sunbonnet and a pink flannel blanket. He looks miserable. Karen laughs.

"You should have seen Aunt Jane's face when she looked in to see the baby!" she says. Aunt Jane and Uncle Billy are Patty's parents and friends of our mother and father, not really our aunt and uncle. They live about a half mile away. I can't say much—it's Karen's day to play with Jeff. But I feel really itchy all over, seeing him crammed into that baby carriage. I walk along beside Karen until we get near the house.

Then, as if he senses he's nearing home and can't stand it another second, Jeff bolts, and blankets, baby bottle, rattle, and buggy go flying. And so does Jeff, the sunbonnet slipped under his chin like a beard of lace.

"That's so cruel!" I say. Karen stops laughing and

squints at me, looking as if I've slapped her.

"What's cruel?" she asks.

"Stuffing a big dog in a baby buggy like that! How'd you get him in there, anyway?"

She shrugs. "I just stood on the step with the baby buggy in front of me, patted the mattress, and he hopped in," she says.

"Yeah, right!" I say.

"He did!" Karen insists. But I don't believe Jeff would do such a humiliating thing as getting into a baby buggy of his own free will to be laughed at like that.

THE FIRST SIGN
OF TROUBLE

When Jeff is mine again the next day, I can't wait to get him out in the woods to see how he does on the trail. I sling Bobby's old canvas newspaper delivery bag over my shoulder in case we find any interesting animals to bring home. At first Jeff dashes off ahead of me, and I call to him. He comes back immediately, ears up.

"If you go crashing around like that," I say, "we aren't going to see any wild animals." He stares at me with his ears up the whole time, then lowers his head and comes back to my side, putting his nose in my hand.

Jeff has turned out to be not much of a barker. Most of the dogs I know bark "Hello!" and "Hey! Where have you been?" and "What dog is that I smell on you?" But I seldom hear Jeff bark—only that deep serious "Whooof!" when I land a fish.

From that moment on, he walks beside me silently, sniffing the air, ears alert. He sees or smells or hears something up ahead and freezes to the spot, his eyes fixed on a stand of trees. I stop and wait, and sure enough, a couple of squirrels chase each other up the trunk of one oak tree and down the next, their tails flicking. I pat Jeff and whisper, "Good dog!" We stand and watch quietly before going on.

The next time Jeff stops, he stares at the bottom of a well-rotted log. I nudge the log gently with my foot, and a velvety orange salamander scrambles from its underside and stands on top, blinking in the sunlight. I reach into the canvas bag for a jar with holes punched into its lid to put the salamander in to carry home. But the log rolls back into place and the salamander scurries off to hide under a fern.

I scratch Jeff behind the ears, and he licks his chops and sits down for a minute while I put the jar back into the bag.

I am looking for a good place to release the snapping turtles. It has to be near water, but I don't want it to be near the lake because I don't want to be responsible for swimmers being bitten by snapping turtles. And I don't want to put them in my pond near the lake, where there's no cover, and the gulls might carry them off to smash their shells on a rock and eat their insides.

There's another small pond far back in the woods, but I want to be sure it hasn't dried up in the heat wave we've had since school has been out. I don't want to haul the turtles all the way out there and then disappoint them. And truthfully, I'm not certain I remember precisely where this little pond is. Jeff smells the ripe, muddy water before I do. We creep toward the edge quietly, and Jeff freezes again.

I would have missed it if Jeff hadn't spotted it— a green-and-black beauty of a snake curled among the wild strawberry vines in the sunlight in a clearing of the woods, his red tongue darting in and out. He must be four feet long.

I lean forward to grab him behind the head to put him into my sack. Just as I do, Jeff lunges forward, landing stiff-legged on his front legs, and the snake slithers away.

"Hey!" I say. I really want a snake, and that's the best snake I've ever found in the woods. "Why'd you do that?" Jeff licks his chops and sits again, his tongue lolling from the side of his mouth. He has acted so purposefully—I'm sure he warned that snake so it could get away.

I sit down cross-legged in the clearing and rest my elbows on my knees. For the first time I put myself in the place of the animals I try to catch. If I were a beautiful, big green snake, the last place I'd want to be is in someone's newspaper delivery bag, being carried home to be kept in a tank. Life is far more interesting in the woods than on the front porch! One time Bobby tried to stow some garden snakes in his T-shirt, and they latched on to his stomach. Mom had to put her foot against him to get enough leverage to pull them off. Bobby had snakebites all over his stomach, and he was really mad at those garden snakes.

"Well, how do you think the snakes felt?" my mother had asked.

Jeff watches me expectantly.

"Oh, all right!" I say. "I won't bring any more snakes or squirrels or birds or rabbits home to put on the front porch. But you have to help me turn everybody loose." Jeff puts his chin on my shoulder, and we sit there for several more minutes. I feel elated about this decision. Watching the animals in the woods is far more exciting than watching them not move in my tanks and cages.

That night I decide I will also be a different kind of fisherman. I love catching fish, but I really prefer watching them when I let them go to eating them. From now on, I will turn loose every fish I catch.

The next day it's Karen's turn with Jeff again. I feed him early and take him fishing, throwing back every fish we catch. It makes my heart sing to watch them flash off and into the weeds. I wonder whether their narrow brush with the frying pan gives them a new appreciation of life.

I bring Jeff up to the house before Karen comes to the kitchen to make breakfast. Karen gets up at about nine and eats breakfast quickly, then slips out the back door to fetch Jeff from the basement. I don't feel like going to the woods or even swimming until I see where Karen is taking him.

I see them head across the front yard toward the McAndrews house across the road. They go in the front door. I get my book and sit on the porch to keep an eye on things. A little while later they come out of the McAndrews house and head toward the lake.

Other children join up with them, and before

they hit the beach a gaggle of kids surrounds my dog, jostling each other for a spot close enough to put a hand on his collar. The worst part is that Jeff's tail wags as he walks. He seems to be enjoying himself, and a big wad of jealousy sticks in my gullet. I flop back down with my book and try to forget about what Jeff is doing without me, and how much fun he's having. My afternoon is miserable.

We're all just sitting down to dinner after my father gets home from work when there is a knock on the door. It's Lucille Nichols from the house behind ours.

"Is that your big tan-and-black dog?" Cille asks. I look around the table.

"Where?" I ask, feeling panic rise. "Where is he?" I ask Karen.

"It sounds as if it might be," my mother says. "Why, what's happened?"

"Well, he got into Ma's rhubarb patch, and there's not a stalk left for her to make pies with."

This is very serious. Just the other side of the hedge that separates our property from the Nicholses' sits the finest patch of rhubarb in Lackawanna County, and Ma Nichols wins first prize with her rhubarb pies at the Grange Fair every year.

"Did Jeff get away from you?" my father asks, shooting me one of his steely looks.

"He wasn't with me today," I say. "He was with Karen." Everyone's eyes turn toward Karen, whose face has turned a bright red. She blinks as if she's trying not to cry.

"He got away from us when we were swimming," Karen says. "He wasn't gone very long. We came home from looking for him and he was sitting on the front porch steps." She looks up at Cille hopefully. "Are you sure it was Jeff?"

"All I know is this," says Cille. "I came home from work and Verna was trying to calm Ma in the kitchen. She was bawling her eyes out. She said a big tan-and-black dog from over this way dug up her entire rhubarb patch and it's ruined for the summer."

I stand and push my chair back from the table.

"May I be excused?" I ask. Without waiting for an answer I run from the dining room and down to the basement. There I discover Jeff with incriminating dirt on his nose and feet. And, more significantly, I also find the reason he might have done such a terrible thing as to dig up Ma Nichols' rhubarb patch.

Jeff's nails have been painted a hot pink—not just one nail on one foot, but all five nails on all four feet—twenty toenails painted hot pink! I'm sure he dug up the rhubarb for revenge. I march back upstairs to confront Karen.

"What did you do to get Jeff to let you paint his toenails?" I demand hotly. I stand beside Karen as she fills the kitchen sink with water to wash the dishes. She shrugs her shoulders and swishes her hands in the soapy water.

"You've been mistreating him." My voice is too loud. "That's why he misbehaved!" Karen doesn't answer immediately. When she does, she looks over her shoulder at me as if she pities me.

"I painted his nails when he was having a nap," Karen says. "He didn't mind a bit. In fact, he liked it."

"Yeah, right!" I say.

"He did!" she insists. "He stretched his feet out and put them against my leg so I could get at his nails better."

I shake my head and stomp off. My mother calls to me a while later to stop sulking and come down to dry the dishes.

BEST-DRESSED DOG

My father is pretty angry.

"If we can't have a dog without annoying the neighbors," he says, "we aren't going to have a dog." His words make my heart ice over.

"He won't annoy the neighbors," I say. "I'll keep him on a leash when we go fishing or into the woods. I'll keep my eyes on him." I look over at Karen.

"Me too!" she says. My father doesn't look convinced.

"One more incident," he says, "and that dog is going to the farm." I'm not sure where the farm is, but it doesn't sound good. When my father speaks in that tone of voice, you don't ask questions. I don't think I want to know anything about the farm at all.

I try to puzzle out why Jeff has misbehaved. I can't really blame it on Karen, although it was a terrible indignity for him to have his toenails painted hot pink. All I know is that Jeff has made me feel like I have a real purpose. I feel as if this summer will last forever, if only I have Jeff with me.

I like to think he grew tired of all those kids hanging on him, and that he slipped away while they went swimming. Karen told me a dozen kids searched the little patch of woods down by the water for nearly an hour, but they found no sign of him.

Karen and I agree that we can afford no more bad behavior, and so we think about how to keep Jeff out of trouble. Also, our grandmother Mema Fisher is coming to visit for a week with her little collie, Missie, and we have to figure out a way to entertain them.

"We could have a fishing contest," I suggest.

"How's that going to keep Jeff and Mema and Missie occupied?" Karen asks. "I hate fishing." Karen has very fair skin that the sun burns quickly. She has to swim wearing a T-shirt and otherwise doesn't go out in the sun unless she has to.

"I know!" says Karen. "A fashion show!" I groan. "We can dress up the dogs so they look like their owners," Karen says. Patty is having lunch with us. She and Karen eat peanut butter and marshmallow sandwiches. I'm eating a cream cheese and olive sandwich, lining up the uneaten crusts on the side of my plate.

"That's a terrible idea!" I say.

"Jeekers creekers!" says Patty, flicking her long braids over her shoulders and pushing her heavy glasses up onto the bridge of her nose. "I think it's a good idea!" "Jeekers creekers" is Patty's favorite expression. I love Patty, and so I agree. We decide to have the fashion show on the community dock the following Saturday afternoon.

The next day we sit at the dining room table and print invitations with purple pencils on red construction paper cut into the shapes of hats.

FASHION SHOW—BRING YOUR DOG DRESSED UP LIKE YOU! Karen writes on her sombrero-shaped invitation. WIN A PRIZE!

"A prize?" I say. "What's the prize going to be?" Karen dabs the tip of her purple pencil on her tongue and thinks for a moment.

GRAND PRIZE, she writes. FREE DOG-SITTING WHILE YOU TAKE A WEEK'S VACATION!

Lots of people say they'll come: Harriet

McAndrews will dress up her Chihuahua, Chico. Dale Van Wert will bring his little dachshund, Cindy. Aunt Jane and Uncle Billy say Patty may bring their boxer, Kurt. Mema will enter Missie. And, of course, we have big plans for what Jeff will wear.

Mema and Missie arrive with my father when he comes home from work Thursday evening. Mom makes our favorite at-home celebration dinner: shrimp and macaroni salad. Mema hugs each of us and tells us how much we've grown. My head almost reaches her shoulder, a good two inches higher than last time we measured.

I run down to the basement to get Jeff, and Mema admires him in the front yard.

"Well, he surely is a big dog," she says mildly. She doesn't sound as impressed as I think she might. Missie comes over to sniff Jeff and turns away again to sit beside Mema, her bushy tail wrapped delicately around her feet in the same self-satisfied way that cats sit.

Jeff goes down on his elbows and gives a playful growl in an attempt to entice Missie into a game. She gives him a frosty glare and lies down. Jeff nudges her with his nose and Missie sighs. She's not interested.

The evening passes in a jumble of talk, with all of us kids surrounding Mema at the table after dinner as she sips her tea. Missie sits under the dining room table all through dinner and dessert.

"Bobby hasn't had a rash or asthma attack all summer," I announce. My mother cocks her eyebrow. "Maybe he's over his allergies." I'm taking advantage now, pressing the point. "Having Missie indoors hasn't bothered him at all," I go on. "Can we let Jeff in?"

"Please? Please?" sing Karen and Charlie in chorus. "Dr. Speicher says I'll get over my allergies," says Bobby. "Maybe this is the summer that I'll get better!"

My mother looks dubious, but she has no resistance in the face of fairness.

"I suppose so," she says. "But no rough-housing. I mean it."

Jeff and Missie lie in the middle of the floor when we move into the living room to continue telling Mema about our latest accomplishments and news. Karen and I talk excitedly about the fashion show. Jeff looks as if he's never spent a night of his life anywhere but lying curled up on the floor, surrounded by his loving family.

Mema helps us plan the menu for the fashion show: lemonade, deviled eggs, celery stuffed with peanut butter, and cookies. I am more enthusiastic somehow, with Jeff in the family midst. Everything seems perfect and I want time to stand still so that it will remain this way always.

On Saturday morning Karen and I squeeze lemons in the kitchen, waiting for Patty to come help us. Mema is on the screened back porch sitting on the glider with another afghan in her lap. She's working on a square with a cornflower blue center. Missie lies curled at her feet, one eye open for Jeff, who pokes her with his nose every time he has the chance. Patty comes to the back door and squeals when she sees them.

"Mema!" says Patty. "I've missed you!" Patty is Mema Fisher's favorite of all our friends.

"I guess we'd better get the cookies started," Mema says, putting the afghan away in the basket beside the glider. Patty pulls a stool up to the kitchen counter, and Mema puts the electric mixer in front of her.

Dale comes by in his golf cart to see how we're doing. Dale is twelve, and he likes to go everywhere with us. We take him out in the rowboat, and he comes when we have cookouts at the stone fire-place in the backyard, and sits with us down by the beach where we spend summer afternoons jumping in and out of the water. I hear his crutches as he comes up the sidewalk, and Cindy barks at the back door. Cindy goes everywhere with Dale.

"How ya doin'?" Dale shouts. I hold the door open for him, trying not to get batter on the doorknob.

"Come on in and take a load off your brain," I say. That's our usual greeting.

"So what's that mutt of yours going to wear in the fashion show?" Dale asks as we pull up a chair for him at the far end of the kitchen. "A halo?" He slaps his knee and laughs his head off.

"Hey!" he says. "How about if I judge the contest?"

"You can't!" I answer. "You're entering Cindy! I can't because I'm entering Jeff."

Since everyone else who is coming to the dog show has a dog entered, we agree that Bobby can be the judge.

We load Dale's golf cart with a cooler and picnic hamper. We put the food on the picnic table in the shade on the far end of the beach, and people begin to arrive with beach towels and folding canvas chairs, which they line up on the grass near the end of the dock. Everyone is here but my father, who has to work.

Karen wants to be the emcee, and she walks out onto the dock wearing her bathing suit and a beach towel draped over her shoulders in her favorite Superman style. The crowd applauds and Karen bows, then raises her arms. I dash up to the tree at the edge of the woods where I've tied Jeff out of sight in his costume.

"Ladies and gentlemen!" Karen shouts into an eggbeater she uses as a microphone. I'm arranging everyone in alphabetical order for the parade out onto the dock. It takes me a while to realize Karen hasn't said anything more. I look up in time to see her run down the ramp toward me. She thrusts the eggbeater into my hand and runs back out to the end of the dock. She releases her towel just before she jumps into the water, and it flutters to the dock. It's not until she lands with a huge splash that I realize she has chickened out and I will have to be the emcee.

This isn't at all what we've planned. I am supposed to lead Jeff out in his costume, which consists of Bobby's swimming trunks and T-shirt and baseball cap, and his mirrored Elvis Presley sunglasses.

"Welcome to the first annual dog fashion show," I say into the eggbeater, hoping I don't sound as rattled as I feel. "Will the contestants please parade one at a time down the ramp?

"First contestant," I say, attempting to sound like Bert Parks announcing the Miss America Pageant, "is Jeff Fisher, wearing the latest in rock-and-roll beachwear. His T-shirt is Fruit Of The Loom, trunks by J. C. Penney, hat compliments of the Scott Township Volunteer Fire Department. His sunglasses are strictly Elvis!" Everyone laughs and claps politely. I'm disappointed at their reserve. Bobby glares at me for a moment because I haven't asked his permission to borrow Jeff's costume.

But he seems satisfied with the audience's response and bends his head to make notes in his notebook. Jeff walks to the end of the ramp, lifts his leg on the gatepost, and pees all over the inside of Bobby's bathing trunks.

MORE TROUBLE

The adults laugh until they all hold their stomachs and their eyes water. Bobby tries to be a good sport, but his face turns red, and his ears look like flames on the sides of his head.

Mom takes Jeff's leash from me and pulls Bobby's dripping swimming trunks off over Jeff's hind legs. I was disappointed when my father said at breakfast that he had to work today, but now I'm glad. I remember his voice after the rhubarb incident, which is only a little more than a week in the past. "One more incident," he said. One more incident. I wonder whether this counts as an "incident."

Without saying a word, my mother leads Jeff into the lake and splashes water on his under parts, then swishes the bathing trunks clean. She goes back to her beach chair and holds on to Jeff's leash while I announce the next contestant. She isn't smiling, but I don't think she looks mad.

Bobby looks distracted, but when I call on Missie he gets back to writing in his notebook.

"Next," I say into the eggbeater, "we have Missie Fisher, owned by Mema Fisher and escorted by Charlie Fisher." Charlie leads Missie down the ramp. Missie wears Mema's wide-brimmed straw gardening hat banded by a lavender satin ribbon with a clutch of violets pinned to it. Tied around her middle is Mema's white eyelet apron. Missie has a sweet, delicate face, and she looks just like Mema. Everyone claps and Charlie grins. I look over at my mother, and she is smiling and clapping along with everyone else.

Harriet McAndrews leads Chico, a scrawny little dog with bulging eyes, out to the edge of the ramp. Harriet has curly hair the color of tomato juice and freckles that look like pickle relish. Like Karen, she has to wear a T-shirt over her bathing suit to keep the sun from burning her shoulders.

Chico's costume is one of those little paper umbrellas from a party drink fastened to his collar so it sticks out over his head, and a tiny paper hula skirt tied around his middle. Everyone laughs and claps some more. Chico sniffs where Jeff has peed and then lifts his leg on the same spot. But people don't look nearly as amused. They raise their eyebrows and make strange shapes with their mouths, as if they're disgusted.

My mother's head is turned toward Aunt Jane, and I can't read her reaction. I wonder whether she'll tell Daddy about Jeff's misbehavior, or whether it'll be lumped together with stories about kids'—and dogs'—behavior.

Next comes Kurt led by Patty. Kurt wears Uncle Billy's hound's-tooth wool porkpie hat, and stuck under his upper lip is a cigar. A blue-and-red polka-dot bow tie is tied under his chin. He looks just like Uncle Billy, who owns the pharmacy in Jermyn. And Kurt has the manners not to pee on the gatepost.

Last is Dale's dog, Cindy, led by Claire, Dale's friend who lives across the street from him. Claire has dressed Cindy in a doll's costume that fits her perfectly, right down to the sunbonnet tied under her chin. Cindy does not look a bit like Dale—more like Claire's little sister, Janice.

Bobby deliberates for a while and then gives the prize to Chico. It's my turn to be disgusted. I guess it's too much to hope that Jeff might actually win, since he's peed all over the judge's swimming trunks.

When we're having lemonade and cookies, Mrs. McAndrews says to Mom, "We really are going on vacation in a week. Are you sure it's all right to leave Chico with you?"

A little cloud passes over Mom's face. Missie and Jeff are two dogs more than she wants living at our house.

"Well," Mom says, "I guess since the girls said they'd take care of the winner, they'll have to honor their commitment."

Good, I think. Karen can paint Chico's toenails and I can have Jeff with me all day every day. Maybe then he won't misbehave and Dad will see what a wonderful dog he is and he'll forget that Jeff has only one more chance before he's sent to the farm.

"Karen!" Mom calls. "Suzanne! Will you come here for a minute, please?" Karen is jumping off the dock with Harriet and Patty. They do somersaults into the water and scramble back up onto the dock to jump again, pretending not to hear. But since I've been standing practically right beside Mom and Mrs. McAndrews, eavesdropping, I can't very well pretend I haven't heard.

"You girls need to talk to Mrs. McAndrews and

find out when they're going away and when they'll be back. Get Chico's leash and bowls and some of his dog food."

"Wait!" I say. Karen jumps from the end of the dock again. "This whole prize idea was Karen's." I want to get back to fishing and out into the woods with Jeff. I have to let those snapping turtles loose and then find places to release all of the other animals on the screened porch.

"You know Karen doesn't like dogs as much as you do," Mom says. "She'll never remember to feed him and walk him. But I know you'll do a good job. After all, you went along with the plan."

Before I have time to contemplate how much I'm not looking forward to taking care of Chico for a week, disaster strikes.

I'm still standing with Mom and Mrs. McAndrews when Bobby comes storming up from the water. He takes me by the arm and pulls me away so our mother can't hear what he has to say. She doesn't like it when we get mad at each other, and Bobby is really annoyed.

"You have to get my mirrored Elvis sunglasses from your dog," he says. His face and ears get red all over again.

Oh my gosh! I've forgotten all about them!

"And they'd better not be scratched." As he talks, he gets madder and his voice rises. "And those were my favorite swimming trunks!"

"Those swimming trunks were really old!" I say.

"It doesn't matter—they're my best ones. How can I wear them now?" I know I was wrong not to ask Bobby's permission, even if they are last year's swimming trunks and are way too small for him, like my old bathing suit is for me. Bobby looks as if he's near tears.

"Okay," I say. "I'm really sorry I didn't ask you. I'll get your sunglasses and T-shirt and hat. But keep your voice down." I should have given his Elvis glasses back a lot sooner, but I hadn't given them another thought in the excitement after the fashion show, and having to set out the cookies and lemonade and other things for people to eat.

I saunter over to the grove of trees where I tied Jeff after the fashion show so he wouldn't get into trouble and I could keep an eye on him. There, lying on the ground, is his leather collar—empty. Beside it are the sunglasses and hat, right where I left them. But the T-shirt is gone with Jeff. He was here not two minutes ago, last time I checked on him. Jeff has mastered the art of the silent disappearance.

My first thought is that Bobby will be angry and will do something to get even with me. But Dougie is talking to him and he doesn't seem to notice that Jeff is gone.

I don't say a word to anyone. I put the hat and sunglasses on and head back down to the dock. I find my moccasins, pull them on over my wet feet, and take off through the woods at a run, looking for Jeff.

The farm! I think. *Dad will send Jeff to the farm!* I look all afternoon in every place Jeff and I have visited together in the woods. But he is gone.

I manage to keep his disappearance a secret simply by not saying anything when I get home. Before supper I take his bowl of food down to the basement, and say nothing when I come back. I wash my hands and set the table. I give Bobby back his hat and sunglasses. I know it's just a matter of time before he demands that I hand over his T-shirt too, but he seems to have forgotten about it.

Jeff doesn't come back the next day, and I run desperately through the woods calling his name and whistling my best baseball game whistle. The same image of Jeff dead beside the road the day we found him plays on my mind. I'm sick. I can't eat.

We are just sitting down to supper when Mr. Wilmot, a farmer who lives about three miles across country from us, pulls up in his hay truck. His daughter, Nancy, is in my class at school. I sometimes go to their house on Saturdays in the winter, and we ice-skate on their pond and eat spaghetti for dinner. Nancy's mother is a terrific cook. Dad goes out to invite Mr. Wilmot in.

"I can't stay," he says, standing beside the dining room table and turning his straw hat in his hands. "Ruth'll have my supper on the table, too. I just brought back a tan-and-black dog Ruth seems to think belongs to you. I got a bird dog in season, and he and about a dozen other dogs were hanging around the barn like a bunch of love-struck teenagers. You might want to keep an eye on him for a while. I usually shoot dogs that run loose on my farm."

My heart is in my throat. Without even asking to be excused, I run from the table, out to Mr. Wilmot's truck, where Jeff lies tied in the bed atop a pile of hay. I throw my arms around his neck and bury my face in his fur, which smells sour, like silage and cow manure. I am both immensely relieved to see him and very anxious. *The farm*, I keep thinking. *They shoot dogs at Mr. Wilmot's farm!* Jeff makes a funny little whine in his throat, and I guess he's glad to see me, too. I unhook the chain from around his neck and help him stand.

He's a sad sight. His ears are shredded at the edges and covered with scabs. His legs and face are crisscrossed with cuts, as if he's been fighting with other dogs. He looks like he hasn't eaten in a month. He can barely walk, and his eyes look glassy.

I take him to the basement with a bowl of fresh water. His food is already there. He walks slowly and with a limp. He lies on his bed and closes his eyes, without eating or drinking. I pet him and he raises his head to lick my hand.

"I don't know what's going to happen, boy," I whisper. A tear falls onto my arm. I wipe my eyes dry quickly on my T-shirt and run back up to the dining room.

After Mr. Wilmot leaves, my father is ominously quiet through the rest of the meal.

"You'd better keep that dog tied up or locked in the basement," he says. "I mean it. One more of his tricks and he'll be gone."

DOG'S GONE

While the threat of the farm is the most serious consequence of Jeff's adventure, it is not the only one.

I have to save my allowance to replace Bobby's Elvis sunglasses, which are scratched, and his T-shirt, which is gone. It will take a whole month. I won't be able to buy any books, and I've been saving for a new bell for my bicycle.

The next morning Mom goes down to the basement to do laundry. She likes to shake out the sheets from the washing machine and hang them to dry in the sunlight because she says it makes them smell fresh.

When she comes in from hanging the sheets, she sits down in the kitchen chair and bends over to inspect her ankles.

"Suzanne!" she yells. I look up from my book, which I have nearly finished, and see her scratching at her ankles. "That dog has fleas. I have bites all over my legs!" she splutters. My mother hates insects of all kinds. Snakes she can handle, but the only things that rattle her nerves of steel are insects.

"Oh my gosh!" I say. The skin on her ankles is red-speckled and puffy.

"Run up and get the calamine lotion, will you, please?" she asks. I get it from the medicine chest, and she spreads it on her ankles until it looks as if she wears chalky pink socks.

"We'd better get some flea shampoo and I'll give Jeff a bath," I say.

Charlie and Bobby have gone to work with my father today, and Karen is at Patty's. So we jump into the car and drive into Jermyn. Mom isn't talking, and she drives like a demon. We go straight to the hardware store on Rushbrook Avenue. I wait in the car. Mom comes out with two bottles: one is a commercial brand of flea shampoo and the other contains a milky brown liquid. She drives straight back home at a fearsome clip. She helps me haul the round galvanized tub from the garage into the backyard, and we hook up the hose.

"You wash the dog," she says. While I get Jeff from the basement, she measures two ounces of the brown liquid into the glass tank of a pump sprayer and fills it the rest of the way with water. The brown liquid forms evil-looking white clouds in the water. My mother folds a handkerchief into a triangle and ties it to cover her nose and mouth before she goes down to the basement like a storm trooper to do battle with the fleas.

Jeff doesn't mind swimming, but he isn't at all fond of bathwater. I hose him off until his fur is soaked and apply the shampoo, which smells something like kerosene. I think maybe it burns the cuts on his ears and legs because he keeps shaking and trying to pull away. The fleas jump from his back like rats abandoning a sinking ship. I feel them pinging off my skin as they leap for dear life. I rinse Jeff and lather him again. Flea corpses float in the metal tub.

After the final rinse, Jeff races around the yard, flipping over onto his back every few minutes to kick his legs into the air, snort, and rub his nose in the grass. It's almost as though he hasn't expected to survive his bath.

When my mother has finished spraying the basement, she goes into the house and pours each of us some lemonade and we sit under the trees sipping from our sweating glasses while Jeff licks the clean from his feet.

"I think maybe we'd better not tell Daddy about the fleas," she says. "I'm not sure he's over the last fiasco." I nod, trying to seem nonchalant, but I am really grateful, because what Jeff doesn't need is more trouble. "And," she says, pausing as if trying to choose her words carefully, "I'm a little worried that you're getting too attached to that dog."

"What do you mean?" I ask. "I've wanted a dog more than anything . . ."

"He is just a dog," my mother says. "It's okay to be fond of him. *I'm* fond of him. But you're so focused on him . . ." Her voice trails away.

"Mom, he's not 'just a dog' to me. He's my only friend."

"Just so you think of other things besides Jeff," she says, looking a little uncomfortable.

"I do—I still love to fish and play baseball. And Jeff cured me of daydreaming. That's good, isn't it?" She smiles and lightly tosses an ice cube in my direction. The afternoon is so warm it seems to melt in midair.

After Jeff's visit to the Wilmot farm, I take him

everywhere on a leash. I never let him off until we're in the thick of the woods or out on the dock fishing, where I'm aware of him every second. I think about what a good thing it is that I've given up daydreaming so I can keep my eye on him. For about a week he's a perfect angel. But I never relax my guard.

Then the time I've been dreading—the week of Chico-sitting—is upon us. Karen and I make several trips across the road to Harriet's house and bring back Chico's bed, blanket, bones, chew toys, leash, harness, bowls, dog food, and finally, Chico himself. Harriet cries as we carry him off, wrapped in a towel so he won't get a chill. Chico quivers. He doesn't stop quivering all day.

Karen is more help with Chico than I thought she'd be. She can paint Chico's nails twice a day and he doesn't mind. Karen tries her Ginny Doll clothes on the quaking Chico out on the picnic table in the backyard. She wraps him in the towel again and carries him around for a while like a baby in a blanket with his face peering out from the triangular opening at the top. Karen likes playing mother, and she's delighted to have a real live baby.

"I don't think we'd better leave Chico in the basement," she says at supper.

"Why not?" Mom asks.

"It's too cold!" Karen says. "I'll keep him in our room. He hardly has any hair at all. I don't think he'll make Bobby sick."

"I don't know . . ." says Mom. Dad is away on a business trip. Karen would never ask if our father had been sitting at the head of the supper table.

"It would be terrible if the McAndrewses came home to find Chico sick!" Karen says. She can be very persuasive. Mom agrees, and Karen takes Chico to our room. He is asleep on her bed when we turn out the light.

In the middle of the night Karen starts yelling.

"Mom!" she hollers. "Mom! Come quick!" She sounds panicked. Karen is pretty tough—nothing much bothers her, except wrinkles in her socks and certain shades of pink. I am alarmed by her tone of voice.

"What's the matter?" I ask, sitting up.

The light snaps on and Karen is out of bed like a shot, hopping up and down and pulling off her blue baby doll pajamas.

"He wee-weed on me!" she shouts, her voice cracking. Mom comes in and changes Karen's bed and gives her clean pajamas.

"I need to take a bath—quick!" she says, her voice quaking. She's still hopping around the room, stark naked and shivering. Chico sits on the end of Karen's bed, watching all of this with his weird bulgy eyes, doing his best to look innocent.

"Take Chico down to the basement," says Mom, nodding her head at me. "Quietly!" She goes to run the bathwater. Karen insists on remaining in the tub with the hot water running for half an hour.

Chico goes quietly to the basement. He doesn't shake once. He probably knows he's gone one step too far. And I think he realizes he's wasting his time trying to get sympathy from me. He doesn't make a sound when I leave him. He just looks at Jeff curled up on his bed of old beach towels and climbs onto the pile beside him. Jeff, looking slightly offended, gets up and goes over near the furnace to sleep on the bare floor.

When Karen and I finally get back into bed, it's 4:00 a.m.

The next morning I get up at six-thirty to go fishing. I go down the steps from the garage and stand in the doorway to the front part of the basement, which consists of the laundry room and rows of shelves where my mother stores her sewing machine and fabrics, canned goods, our winter clothes, things for the church rummage sale, luggage, and who-knows-what-all else.

I call softly for Jeff to come. But I can tell by the dead stillness in the basement that it's empty. Usually I hear Jeff's tail thump the floor or his toe-nails click as he jumps up and down with excitement, waiting for me to open the door.

I flip the light switch on and walk through the door that leads into the second large room, which contains my father's woodworking shop in the back part of the basement. I turn on that light. At one end my father's shop stands neatly in order with his equipment clean and sparkling, tools hung in rows on pegboard above the bench, nothing out of place.

At the other end stands disaster. A large pile of splinters and wrecked train equipment, twisted train track and crushed miniature buildings make me think at once of an earthquake.

When Bobby was a baby, my father began to construct an elaborate landscape for the miniature locomotive train set that had been his when he was a boy. Each year for ten years, Dad expanded the track bed, constructed papier-mâché mountains, and artfully covered them with small trees made from twigs. He fashioned a river of aluminum foil, fitted a town with handcrafted wooden buildings, made pastures of green felt with plastic cows grazing on them, and cut a large mirror to form a lake that the train skirted.

My father's pride and joy stood on a platform about three feet above the floor. Now it is a jumble of devastation beneath two basement windows set high in the wall.

It seems impossible that the dogs—even a big dog like Jeff—could have climbed out through those windows, which my father leaves open to keep the basement from smelling musty.

It hasn't occurred to me that the object of Jeff's affection at the Wilmot farm might still attract him a whole week later. And I was sure he'd learned his lesson the first time. It's hard to imagine how those two dogs could have created so much damage without sledgehammers. I am sure the whole thing was Chico's idea.

DOG VISITS FARM

I creep back upstairs to our bedroom and awaken Karen to tell her Jeff and Chico are gone. She begins to cry.

"Harriet won't speak to me ever again, not for as long as I live!" she says between sobs.

"We'll find them," I say, wanting her to stop crying before everyone in the house wakes up and discovers the havoc Jeff and Chico have wreaked while escaping from the basement.

"Why don't you go out on your bicycle and look around the neighborhood," I suggest. "I'll look in the woods and down around the lakefront."

"What time is it?" Karen asks. She's never in her life gotten out of bed so early, even on a school day.

"Eight," I lie. It's six forty-five.

We look all morning, both of us on our bicycles. I mostly walk mine along paths in the woods and down among the docks, calling Jeff's name and whistling my famous baseball game whistle.

I think about what my mother said about loving Jeff too much. I don't understand how I could possibly love him less. I wonder whether the quantity of love you have in your heart is voluntary. Maybe it's something like changing the subject when you find yourself daydreaming. You learn how to love someone, and when it gets to be "too much" you stop. I can't imagine it.

Just before noon I decide to go home and try putting the train platform back together. If I can fix it, maybe we won't have to tell our parents what happened.

Down in the basement I tug at one of the pieces of plywood that made the base. I can lift only one corner of it, and I'm not strong enough to hold it for more than a few seconds. The train tracks are bent and twisted together. I try to straighten a piece. I can't do it with my hands, so I go to my father's workbench, climb up to the pegboard on the wall behind it, and take down a hammer. The track breaks under the hammer. We definitely will have to tell Mom. I imagine my father coming home tired from his business trip only to hear more bad news about Jeff.

At lunchtime my mother notices Karen isn't carrying Chico around wrapped in a towel. And Jeff isn't sitting by the back door with his nose up against the screen as he usually does when we're eating lunch.

"I haven't seen either one of the dogs all day," she says as she makes our sandwiches in the kitchen. "Have you?"

Karen and I look at each other. Neither of us speaks. We both look down at the bread and mustard and bologna my mother has spread out on the cutting board on the kitchen counter.

"I want mayonnaise, not mustard," says Karen, stalling.

"Please," says Mom.

"Please," says Karen.

"So?" Mom says, shifting her eyes from the sandwiches to mine.

"They're gone," I say. Karen nudges my ankle with her bare foot, and I give her a look back.

My mother glances up from her sandwich making. "What do you mean, 'they're gone'?"

"They got out through the basement window last

night," I say. "Right after they wrecked the train set. Daddy is going to be really mad."

"And Harriet won't ever speak to me again," Karen says, her lips quivering. She realizes we're caught.

"Have you looked for them?" Mom asks.

I nod. "We've been out looking all morning."

Mom doesn't say anything for a minute.

"Do you want mustard?" she asks, and I nod. She arches her brow.

"Please," I manage to add.

"After lunch we'll go down and have a look at the train set," she says. "Then we'll search for those two dogs in the car. They're probably over at the Wilmot farm. First, let's eat our sandwiches outside at the picnic table."

We troop out to the backyard with our glasses of milk and sandwiches. No one says much as we swish at the flies and eat. When we're finished, Karen and I take the plates and glasses in to wash in the sink while Mom goes down to the basement to have a look.

"Your father will be furious," she says when she comes back upstairs. "Those trains are ruined. All of his hard work . . ." Her brow is wrinkled and she looks shaken. "How did Chico get out through a window set that high in the wall?"

"For a little dog he can jump really high," Karen says.

"What do you think Daddy will do?" I ask, trying to swallow the lump in my throat.

"I don't know," she says. "We should find those dogs before they get into more trouble." Mom telephones Mrs. Wilmot, but there is no answer. We get into the car and drive over to the farm. Nobody is at the house, and we don't see a sign of the dogs around the barn. We ride around most of the rest of the afternoon with the windows rolled down, calling and whistling.

We stop at Kiesel's Corner Store in the village of Montdale and buy some milk. We stop at Micky York's gas station, the Methodist Church, where the minister is mowing the grass, and everywhere else we can think to stop. We describe Chico and Jeff and ask whether anyone has seen them. Every single person makes the same bad joke. "You mean Mutt and Jeff?" they ask, hardly able to contain their laughter.

Finally we're worn out and turn the car for home. I rest my head on my arms, folded on the frame of the open front-seat passenger window. The sun is warm on my cheek, and the wind blows through my hair and fills the car with the sweet scent of freshly mown hay. I pray that Jeff will be there when we get home, and that Mom will find a way to get the train set fixed without telling Daddy. In return I will give up fishing or baseball—both—anything!

When we get home, the telephone is ringing. Mom dashes into the house and picks it up on about the eighth ring.

"Hello?" she says. "Yes, Ruth. We were over there a while ago and . . . Oh." She waits while Mrs. Wilmot speaks, and then says, "How much?" Another pause, then: *"How much?"* And I know we're really in trouble. She puts the receiver down.

"Mr. Wilmot shot four dogs that were hanging around his barn all week," she says. I gasp. "Not Jeff," she adds quickly. "He's locked up in their shed with Chico. She said if we come over and get them right now, Mr. Wilmot won't shoot them." My stomach gives a sickening lurch and I feel sweat bead on my scalp. I give an involuntary shiver. *"And . . .* he wants fifty dollars to replace two windows the dogs broke to get into the barn."

"A window costs that much?" I ask.

"Reid Wilmot is known for his bird dogs. Now they're going to have mutts—the puppies will be part Jeff's. He usually gets twenty-five dollars a puppy. He is *not* happy."

I can't say a word. My mouth feels glued shut, and my heart hammers inside my chest. The news my father hears when he gets home will be all bad. I don't want to think about how he'll react.

We get back into the car and drive first to the bank in Jermyn so Mom can get fifty dollars in cash to give to Mr. Wilmot. Fifty dollars is a *lot* of money. We drive back over to the Wilmots' farm. Mrs. Wilmot sits under a tree in the front yard fanning herself with a folding paper fan. A frosty pitcher of ice water sits in the grass beside her feet. Next to it are five different-colored aluminum cups stacked one inside the other. Near the edge of the road is a large wooden table loaded with bushel baskets of tomatoes, peppers, and the summer's first ears of corn. A cardboard sign hangs from the table on baling twine. CORN 50 CENTS A DOZEN, it reads. PEPPERS, SQUASH, TOMATOES 5 CENTS APIECE.

As we get out of the car, her daughter, Nancy, comes out the front door of the house wearing shorts and a peasant blouse with elastic around the shoulders, arms, and midriff. Her long, wavy blond hair is pulled back into a ponytail, and on her feet she wears pink ballet slippers. Nancy takes ballet lessons, and she never lets you forget it for one second.

"Want to see my lamb?" she asks, doing a plié on the top step of the porch. I don't really want to do much of anything except get Jeff, go home, and have this day over with.

"Go ahead," says Mom. "I want to talk to Mrs. Wilmot."

Nancy takes Karen and me out to the shed behind the house where a lamb that's almost the size of Jeff stands grazing within a small fenced area.

"Come here, Trudy," says Nancy. She leans over the wire fence and holds out her hand, wiggling her fingers. Trudy's white wool is tightly curled, and her face and feet are black. She bucks and kicks, then trots over and takes Nancy's fingers into her mouth, sucking loudly.

"Want to try?" Nancy asks. "It feels funny." I nod dumbly and stick my hand over the fence. I usually love going to Nancy's, feeding the animals, playing with the babies, and exploring the barn. But today I feel immune to cute animals, even when Trudy takes my fingertips into her pink toothless mouth and sucks at them gently. It's an odd, sweet sensation. Karen quickly thrusts her hands behind her back and watches dubiously. Karen doesn't much like getting dirty or touching strange things.

A few minutes later, Mom calls us. Mrs. Wilmot is loading a bag of corn into the back of our car as we come around to the front of the house. "Let me get you some cucumbers," she says. She goes through a gate in the fence behind Trudy's pen and comes back with four cucumbers hammocked in her apron.

Nancy takes Karen and me to a pen out near the barn to get the dogs. We find Jeff curled up near the gate to the pen, sound asleep. Chico is in the corner. He sees Karen and begins to shiver. Karen wraps him in a beach towel she's brought with her and puts him in the car. I snap the leash on Jeff's collar and drag him to his feet. He sleeps all the way home.

When Daddy arrives home looking hot and tired, dinner is almost ready and Mom is busy getting it onto the table. I don't volunteer the information about Jeff, and neither does Karen.

When we're halfway through our meat loaf and ears of corn, Charlie pipes up.

"Dad, Jeff wrecked the trains and ran away and

Mom had to pay fifty dollars to get him back," he says, sounding important. I want to twist his ear.

"Not at the table," says Mom, her brow knotting up again.

"Well, now that I know, you might as well tell me," Daddy says, reaching for the sliced tomatoes. He has been in a pretty good mood until now. It's Friday, and he's happy to be back from another long business trip, home for the weekend.

Mom does all the talking.

"That dog is more trouble than we can afford," my father says when she's finished. "He skulks around without making a sound, and the next thing you know, he's in trouble."

"Daddy," I say, pleading. "It wasn't Jeff's fault!" My father twitches one eyebrow. A man his size can say a lot with one small part of his body.

"Whether it was his fault is immaterial," he says. "We can't afford fifty dollars for that kind of nonsense!"

"We'll pay you back!" I say. Karen nods her head vigorously, her curls bouncing.

"It would take you two years," my father says. Our allowance is twenty-five cents apiece each week for doing chores around the house. "If he gets away again, you'll be paying me back for the rest of your lives."

My mother leans forward. "Ruth Wilmot told me Reid's cousin whose farm is out past Tunkhannock is looking for a dog," she says.

"You've got to give him one more chance!" I say. "Karen and I will take turns with him on the leash whenever he's not in the basement. And I swear we'll pay you back."

Karen and I look at each other. Bobby watches my father closely. Even Charlie sits still.

"So what are you going to do?" asks Bobby. I put my hands over my ears. I can't stand to hear what my father will say. He looks sideways at me. No one says anything for at least a minute. Tears leak from the corners of my eyes and run down my face.

I can't hear anything, but I see Karen's face change—she smiles a huge smile and reaches across her plate for the salad. Dad leans over and gently takes me by the wrist, pulling my one hand away from the ear it covers.

"One more chance," he says. "I—mean—it! Only one chance."

GOOD DOG

Because Karen and I share responsibility for Jeff—and because Mom insists we have to share time with him equally—my sister and I spend more time together than we ever have any other summer.

The McAndrewses come home from their vacation, and Chico goes home to live with them, much to my relief. The next day Karen, Jeff, and I go to the pond so I can find a suitable place to turn the baby snapping turtles loose. Before we leave our yard, I warn her about talking.

"We want to go through the woods so the animals don't even know we've been there," I say. "We'll see a lot more of them if we're really quiet." I show her how to walk on the balls of her feet. Karen wears sneakers and knee socks and she couldn't care less about whether we'll see deer in the woods. But she does try to walk quietly and she manages not to talk.

Karen carries the cardboard box with the turtles and walks behind me while I look for a good spot with quiet water and a nice soft, silty bottom. Jeff runs in and out of the water a few yards away, pouncing and playing and having a grand time. After I say goodbye to the turtles, I call Jeff to put the leash back on him. He's never tried to get away from me when we're in the woods, but I don't want to take any chances. He is wet all over with ripe-smelling mud up to his armpits. Karen holds her nose most of the way home.

As we turn down the path toward our house in the last stretch of woods before the lake, we hear the jingle of the ice cream truck. Karen takes off at a dead run, and Jeff follows, dragging me along behind. Karen bursts into the kitchen, with the two of us on her heels.

"Mom!" shouts Karen, although my mother stands just three feet away, putting the mop and bucket away. She's just cleaned the kitchen floor. "Can we have fifteen cents for a Nutty Bar?"

"You've got dirt all over your feet!" Mom says. "Don't come in here . . ." Then she sees Jeff, who bolts through the doorway, even though he knows he isn't allowed in the house. "Get that dog out of here!" Mom shouts. "He's covered with mud."

At that moment our attention is drawn to something else about Jeff. He hunches forward and humps his back, and his eyes take on a glazed look as his stomach begins to heave.

"Get him out before he—" But before Mom can finish, Jeff urps, and a whole, live frog leaps from somewhere deep in his throat. The frog lands on all four feet and keeps hopping straight for the doorway into the dining room. We are transfixed with amazement for a second or two. Feeling relieved of the burden in his stomach, Jeff wags his tail heartily, splattering mud all over my mother's sparkling kitchen. *"Out!"* Mom shouts. *"Out!"*

I lunge for the frog, which is halfway across the dining room, and Karen grabs Jeff's leash to take him outside. I take the frog down to release him in the lake while Karen ties Jeff to the tree in the backyard. When I come back, my mother puts us to work cleaning the kitchen until it sparkles again.

I worry as I push the wet mop across the floor that this might have blown Jeff's last chance. But that night after supper, as Karen and I wash the dishes, I hear my mother and father laughing in the living room. I hush Karen so we can listen. Mom is telling him about the frog, and they both laugh so hard I decide to quit worrying.

The next day Karen, Harriet, and I are out in the backyard with Chico and Jeff, teaching them tricks. Harriet claims Chico is smarter. He can walk on his hind legs, and he does appear to dance. Jeff can't balance on his hind legs for very long.

"Jeff can shake hands," I say. "Shake," I command, and Jeff sticks his paw out. I taught him that as soon as he came to live with us. "Can Chico do that?"

Harriet shrugs.

"Shake, Chico," she says, as if she really expects him to do it. He just looks at her with his bulging black eyes. Of course Chico can't shake.

At about that time Dale comes along in his golf cart, Cindy sitting in his lap, her dachshund ears riding like sails on the breeze as they lurch across the backyard.

"How ya doin'?" Dale asks as he organizes his crutches to get out of the golf cart.

"Have a seat and take a load off your brain," I say. Dale laughs as if we don't say the exact same thing every time we see each other. We get a chair for him, and he lays his crutches on the ground by his feet.

"We're having a contest to see whose dog is smartest," I explain. "Can Cindy do any tricks?"

"Sure—for a price," says Dale. "Cindy," he commands. Her sweeping ears perk forward, and she jumps back into Dale's lap. "Give us a kiss." Cindy stands on her hind legs in Dale's lap and covers his face with licks.

"Yek!" says Karen with genuine disgust.

"Well, we're doing tricks they already know," I say. "Let's see who can learn a trick the fastest."

We try to teach the dogs to roll over, but for some reason getting them to lie down is a lot harder than teaching them to sit. Dale thinks we have to pull their legs out from under them if they don't lie down immediately. That works with Cindy and Chico, but Jeff seems to think it's an invitation to wrestle.

Jeff and I tumble around on the ground. He has the neck of my T-shirt in his teeth. I laugh—we're all laughing—Jeff growls. It's play growling, not for real.

Suddenly Mr. Bell, the mailman, comes through the hedge, taking his usual shortcut through Ma Nichols' backyard to our house, which is a lot closer than walking the long way around. Mr. Bell must be in a hurry because he walks fast, and seeing him burst through the hedge like that takes us all by surprise.

In a split second, Jeff plants himself in front of Mr. Bell and bares his teeth. His throat vibrates in a menacing growl.

"Jeff!" I call. "Quit that!" In one fluid motion Mr. Bell drops his mailbag, pulls the leather strap from it, and slaps it at Jeff's face. Jeff lunges. I don't think he means to bite Mr. Bell, or he would connect. Instead Jeff's teeth snap loudly in the air. Mr. Bell starts slashing the belt at him. The end of it makes a cracking noise as it lands on Jeff's nose. Jeff yelps, but instead of cowering he goes after Mr. Bell with renewed ferocity.

"No!" Karen screams at Mr. Bell. Jeff grabs Mr. Bell's pants leg and holds on. Mr. Bell begins kicking wildly, and Jeff's feet leave the ground.

"Get Mom!" I say to Karen, and I try to grab Jeff's collar. Mr. Bell slashes wildly with the leather strap, which strikes me several times, burning my arms and cheek and bringing tears to my eyes. "For Pete's sake!" I shout. "Cut that out!"

Karen lights out across the backyard, yelling for

Mom at the top of her lungs.

"What do you think you're doing?" Mom says to Mr. Bell, who keeps right on slashing at Jeff and me. My mother can be formidable when she's protecting us.

"That dog came after me and bit me," he says, his breath coming in gasps from the exertion.

"He did not!" I say. "You surprised us, and Jeff just growled. You hit him first!"

"Stop it!" Mom says, grabbing Mr. Bell's arm in mid-slash. "What's the matter with you, whipping children and a dog like that?"

Mr. Bell's face is a deep red. He is a tall, skinny man, and his Adam's apple bobs up and down as he struggles to compose himself.

"You ought to be arrested for keeping a vicious dog like that!" he shouts at my mother. "I'm telling the Post Office to put you on general delivery!"

FALLING DOG

The Post Office does *not* put us on general delivery. And for once it isn't Jeff but Mr. Bell who gets in trouble. Afterward he isn't allowed to come through the hedge from Ma Nichols' yard. He has to go around and come up the front walk like everyone else.

Mr. Bell won't speak to Karen and me after that, and we have to put Jeff away every afternoon at about two o'clock, when it's almost time for the mail to be delivered.

But now whenever a stranger approaches, Jeff plants himself between the stranger and Karen and me. The hair on the back of his neck bristles and he growls. He never tries to bite anyone, but people begin to be afraid of him.

Oddly enough, the incident with Mr. Bell softens

our father's heart toward Jeff. For the first time Daddy notices the look of sheer sweetness that comes into Jeff's eyes when he is surrounded by children.

"His eyes look like Hershey's syrup," my father says. He thinks perhaps Jeff is part sheepdog because of the way he herds Karen and me when he thinks we might be in danger.

Late one night, when I have slipped the flashlight under my blanket to read the last part of *Black Beauty* for about the fifth time, I get up to go to the bathroom before I go to sleep. Tiptoeing down the hallway, I hear my mother and father talking in hushed tones in their bedroom, which is next to the bathroom.

I'm not exactly eavesdropping—just trying not to get caught out of bed long after I'm supposed to be asleep. I realize they're talking about me, and so I stand still and listen.

"I've never seen her so happy," says my mother. "She's well adjusted and cheerful. I'm just worried that she's too attached to him."

"I'm afraid he's going to bite someone," my father says. "After something like that incident with Ray Bell you never know . . . A dog gets to be unpredictable once he's gone after somebody."

"Ray Bell provoked him," my mother says.

"It doesn't matter," says my father. "We really have to keep our eye on him."

I take up worrying again because I know Jeff is still living on his very last chance. But things go smoothly enough for a while.

It's a Saturday in August and my father decides to paint the trim around the windows of our house. He has several gallons of dark green paint left over from the renovation of his office building in Scranton, and the house needs a face-lift. Dad goes to the garage and gets out the old, paint-splattered eight-foot stepladder. Its rusty hinges protest loudly as he sets it up alongside the first window.

"Be careful, Bob," my mother says as he climbs the ladder carrying a gallon of paint, two paint-brushes, and an old towel to use as a rag. The can is full except for a quantity he has poured into a small coffee can and given to Bobby to paint the canoe. "You'll need an extension ladder for the second floor," Mom says, and turns to go back into the house.

It's tedious work. My father carefully applies

paint with the smaller brush on the wood next to the windowpane and along the edge of the siding. He uses the larger brush for the center of the window trim. He works slowly, taking care not to get green paint on the white siding. As he finishes each window, he climbs down the ladder carrying the rag, brushes, and paint can, moves the ladder to the next window, and climbs two thirds of the way back up the ladder again.

Karen and I are in the garage helping Bobby paint the canoe. The old wood-and-canvas hull is heavy with layers of paint even after scraping, and every year it seems to spring a new leak. Bobby lovingly sands and oils its teak gunwales several times a year. I'll be glad when he finally gets a car, because then the canoe will be in the water more than it's in the garage.

Mema, who has come to stay with us for the week, sits at the picnic table under the tree in the backyard, beside the garage door. She has her crocheting in her lap, and Missie lies beside her feet. Jeff is tied to the leg of the picnic table. His eyes are closed, but he cocks an ear every time someone speaks.

"Your paint is running in huge drips!" Bobby says

to Karen. "You're getting it on the gunwales!"

"I am not!" says Karen. She doesn't like to be criticized. And she's getting tired and hot.

"You're supposed to paint side to side, the way the boards go," he says. Karen has been painting up and down, and her paint is dripping in heavy ribbons.

"You can paint it yourself, then!" she says, setting her brush on the edge of the paint can. She wipes her hands on an old T-shirt.

"Good!" says Bobby, who is a bit of a perfectionist when it comes to "his" canoe. It was our idea to help him, and he prefers to work by himself. Dad told him to let us help.

Karen throws the rag down and goes off to watch Mema crochet.

Bobby and I paint steadily.

Daddy comes into the garage looking for more rags. While he rummages around in the ragbag, we hear the squeak of the ladder from around the side of the house where Daddy has been painting. It sounds like someone is slowly and stealthily climbing the ladder.

My father runs out of the garage with Bobby and me on his heels. Karen and Mema stand up to follow.

We all round the corner of the house to see Jeff halfway up the ladder. He looks at us, first with surprise in his eyes, and then with the realization that he doesn't know how to get down.

Jeff stands poised, his two front paws on the rung in front of his nose, his hind paws on two different rungs, one above the other. He looks first at my father and then at me, and after the briefest hesitation he jumps, knocking the ladder aside as he goes.

The can of green paint seems to take on a life of its own, leaping into the air, then tumbling end over end in slow motion until it lands directly on Jeff's head. It rolls down his neck and comes to rest on his shoulders, pouring paint in a steady stream as it goes. By the time it lands right side up on the ground it's empty, and Jeff's entire front end and back are coated thickly with green paint. The ladder teeters back and forth and then falls on top of the squirming green dog. Jeff begins to scream.

I've never heard such a desperate sound from any living creature. I can tell by the look on Jeff's face (which is entirely green) that he is about to bolt for the woods. Fortunately, Daddy leaps forward and grabs him first. Jeff keeps yelping, and twists and turns frantically, trying to untangle himself from the ladder and get away. My heart beats wildly, but I'm rooted to the spot. My father manages to hold on to him with his arms, since Jeff's collar seems to be missing.

"Is he all right?" I ask. I'm surprised to hear the shaking in my voice. Daddy talks softly to Jeff, trying to calm him.

"Help me get this ladder off him," he says to Bobby. "Karen, go get the bag of rags from the garage. Suzanne, come here and stand beside him. Don't put your hands out." Jeff's teeth are bared as he struggles. I can tell my father is making a huge effort to keep his voice calm and quiet.

Bobby grabs the ladder, and Daddy keeps hold of Jeff, who bucks and squirms like a bronco in the rodeo. At this point my father also is covered with green paint. Bobby pulls the ladder upright, and Karen reappears with the rags. Jeff stops twisting and jumping and yelping. With the rag in his hand my father wipes at the paint that covers Jeff's eyes, clearing them until they're once again brown surrounded by white.

"Is he all right?" I ask again.

"I think he's mostly scared," Daddy says. His voice is calm, but there is a note in it that alarms me.

It's quiet but not happy—it's almost grim.

Once I realize Jeff is more frightened than hurt, another fear settles over me. I'm afraid Jeff has used up his very last chance, and that once my father realizes it he'll send my dog off to the farm.

We spend the next hour trying to clean Jeff up, using the entire bag full of rags. Missie stays under the picnic table, where she peers out at all of us bending over Jeff, calming him and cleaning him. She looks a little smug, as if getting into trouble is all that she expects of Jeff.

"Why wasn't he tied up?" my father asks as we work, after the initial shock has worn off.

"He was!" I say. "He was under the picnic table— right under Karen's and Mema's feet!" We all look at them. They look at each other and then at Jeff's collar, which is still tied by his leash to the leg of the picnic table. That dog is a regular Houdini!

BACK TO SCHOOL

My father doesn't say a word about last chances, and I don't dare bring it up. Over the next several days I begin to feel as if I can breathe normally again. But I have a strange feeling that Jeff is living on borrowed time. He remains the same color as the canoe and the trim on the house and the doors in my father's office building.

We finish painting the canoe and launch it in mid-August for the first time since the summer before. Bobby needs someone to paddle at the bow, which I'm good at. He and Karen and I spend hours crisscrossing the lake. It's exciting to have something new to do so late in the summer.

Jeff follows us everywhere on the water, swimming with his nose just a few inches from the stern of the canoe. Sometimes he spends the entire day on the lake with us, swimming four or five hours at a time without resting. It's almost as if he finally realizes that if he gets too far away from us we won't be able to keep him. I have a terrible feeling it's already too late. But I don't say anything, because that might make it true.

"Land sakes!" says Mema, who has come for the last two weeks of summer. "It's a wonder that dog's still green after all the time he spends in the lake!"

We've given him several baths, but the paint won't come off and Jeff has developed a rash that nearly drives all of us crazy because of his scratching. The baths have other consequences as well. After Jeff's third bath, when the individual hairs in his fur are just beginning to unstick from each other, Jeff bolts before he's even rinsed, knocking over the galvanized tub as he goes. His feet hit the ground running straight for the lake. I grab his collar and leash and take off after him.

Down at the lakefront I see Jeff's kicking feet before I see the rest of him. He's on his back, and it looks as if he's running with his feet in the air. It isn't until I crest the slope that leads down to the beach that I can see what he's up to.

Something has caused a fish kill in the lake—not a major kill, but enough of one that a couple of dozen dead perch and sunfish, plus a nice-sized bass, lie scattered along the waterline with flies buzzing all over them. Jeff, who hates to be clean and nice-smelling, is rolling in the dead fish, doing his best to smell like he's never had a bath in his life.

I buckle his collar around his neck and snap on his leash, and we walk back up to the house. He smells disgusting, even to me, but he holds his head high and prances along beside me. I think it's his way of letting me know he's going to be himself against all odds.

"Into the tub again!" my mother says, holding her nose and trying not to retch. "I've just about had it with that dog!" Her eyes stream with tears, and she speaks in a tone of voice usually reserved for our most serious offenses. I hurry Jeff off to tie him while I fill the galvanized tub with water. Her words stick with me and that funny feeling in the pit of my stomach refuses to go away.

As I bend over the tub, trying to scrub the stink from Jeff's fur, I realize we will have to leave him in the basement by himself when we go back to school. He can't stay outside because he'll slip his collar and run away again to the Wilmots'. And I have little doubt that Mr. Wilmot would shoot him this time. When I finish, I take Jeff down to the basement and lock him in the laundry room. He still smells. I go upstairs and tiptoe across the back porch and living room, and up the stairs. Walking on the balls of your feet works as well on old wooden floors as it does in the forest.

I go to my parents' bedroom and slip Mom's bottle of Chanel No. 5 into my shorts pocket. Back in the basement, I dab some of it on Jeff, who pulls away and shakes himself until it seems his fur might fly off. He doesn't smell much better, but at least I can walk into the basement without gagging. When my mother comes down to do laundry I hope her first thought won't be, "I've just about had it with that dog!"

As the end of August approaches, I want to hang on to the summer. I don't want to go back to school. I don't want to stop fishing and swimming and walking in the woods with Jeff. I don't want to give up the long days of freedom to go wherever my heart leads me. And for some reason fifth grade has no appeal at all.

Most days a brisk breeze comes up and the sun

shines brightly, outlining everything with a hard, golden edge. It makes you think about how soon the brilliant green leaves will turn red, orange, and yellow, and shortly thereafter the branches of the trees will be black against a gray sky, without any softening of leaves. It makes you want to hold on to every minute of sunlight.

It's almost as if we have to play harder because we don't have much time left until school starts. Kids of all ages play together now, unlike during the rest of the summer, when best friends spend long afternoons at each other's houses. It's the only time during the summer that I am a regular part of the gang of kids in our neighborhood.

We start to need sweatshirts when we get out of the water, which is warmer than it's been all summer. We spend less time swimming and more time playing kick the can and other games because it's too chilly to be comfortable in a wet bathing suit. My mother tells us to put shoes on because it's too cold to go barefoot.

Our neighborhood softball games go from one or two evenings a week to a game every day. Instead of the usual handful of kids, everyone plays—mothers, fathers, grandparents, teenagers, and any kid big enough to pick up a bat. Charlie is one of the youngest players, and he's an excellent runner. The days grow shorter and we play softball as if it's the last game any of us will ever play.

And then, finally, it's Labor Day weekend. Every year at this time I think about hot dogs, hamburgers, and toasted marshmallows. Every year the holiday is tinged with sadness, but this year I'm sad *and* worried. I'm not ready to go back to school. I don't want to get any older. I want things to stay as they are.

We play our Labor Day farewell-to-summer baseball game late in the afternoon on Sunday, with the players' relatives and friends and neighbors watching from canvas-and-wood beach chairs set up in the meadow across the road from the playing field. It's the last game before the summer people head back to town. From now on we'll play with only a handful of players.

The game is tied at the end of the last inning, and we play a tiebreaker, which also is tied. My mother and Mema sit with Jeff and Missie at their feet. My mother has the loop of Jeff's leash around her wrist. The game ends when Jeff breaks free, tears across the road, dragging his leash, and steals the ball.

"Oh well," says Uncle Billy, who is our team's

catcher, "it's getting too dark to see." So we all go home, happy to have the last game end in a tie. My parents let Jeff sit with us around the fieldstone fireplace in the backyard while we have one last summer fire and make s'mores by melting toasted marshmallows and a bar of chocolate between graham crackers. We stay up until after ten o'clock.

A lot of families around the lake move back to town on Labor Day, their cars piled high with picnic chairs, blankets, pillows, clothes, kids, and pets.

Tuesday after the holiday my mother takes Karen and me into town to do last-minute shopping for school. We get new saddle shoes and sweaters to match the skirts Mom has made for us during the summer. We've both outgrown our school clothes from the year before. We also get blue jeans and flannel shirts and new sweatshirts, sneakers, and book bags. With the allowance my father lets us have back after our weekly payments for Mr. Wilmot's broken window, Karen and I each buy a big, bubble-gum-pink eraser and a pencil set.

And then, although we can hardly believe it, the following Monday is the first day of school. My feeling of sadness has turned to dread. The house is in chaos with all four of us getting ready at once. Karen is grouchy because she has to get up at six-thirty, and tears are spilled before breakfast because she wants to wear a skirt and top that my mother says don't match.

Charlie is starting first grade, and you would think he's the world's only boy to go off to school for the first time. The breakfast table is dominated by his questions. "How many pencils should I take?" he asks, spilling out onto the table dozens of pencil stubs he's collected over the previous weeks. "I know how to write already, so I'll probably have to show the other kids how," he says. "The teacher probably will call on me more often, because I can already read." Bobby rolls his eyes.

Somehow we get out the door in time to walk the quarter mile out to Brown Hollow Road to meet the school bus at seven forty-five sharp. Charlie is very excited. He never quits talking from the second we leave the house. He talks about how heavy his book bag is, what he's going to have for lunch, what he'll tell his classmates when his teacher has each of them stand to introduce themselves.

"She'll probably call on me first," he says. "I'll be the tallest kid in the class." Charlie is pretty tall for his age.

I try to listen to him, but am distracted by the

feeling of dread that has plagued me now for many days. And Jeff will have no one to play with while we're gone. Before I left him in the basement, I explained that he'd have to entertain himself somehow until we got home. He was very aloof when I hugged him one last time. He laid his head back down on his pile of beach towels and closed his eyes.

I didn't mention that I hoped he wouldn't get bored and try to sneak out of the basement again. I didn't want to give him any ideas. Mom promised she'd check on him every once in a while and take him for a walk at lunchtime. I think he sensed somehow that things were about to change.

TALE'S END

"Will you?" I hear Charlie say. He and Karen and Bobby are looking at me, waiting for an answer.

"Will I what?"

Charlie looks exasperated. "Bring my milk money down to my teacher before you go to your class!" Mom gave me Charlie's snack money just before we left the house.

"Yes, I'll go with you. Don't worry," I say. But I resume thinking about Jeff and what we'll find to do after school, since it's too cold to swim and the fishing isn't so great in the afternoons at this time of year. I contemplate a mission to the pond.

We get off the bus in front of the beige brick school building and Bobby goes toward the junior high school. Karen, Charlie, and I head for the grade school. I walk to the first grade with Charlie to give the teacher his snack money, then on to my fifth-grade homeroom.

Mrs. Schwartzstrauber is a small, round woman with tight gray curls. She stands smacking a ruler into the palm of her hand at the doorway. I am the last one into the room, and I guess she wants to set the tone for how things will go in her class.

I'm glad to see my classmates—even Nancy, who wears a bright red corduroy jumper with a crisply ironed lace-collared blouse. I always feel frumpy around Nancy, even when she wears blue jeans. Everyone is talking about what they did on their vacation; everyone has on new shoes; everyone has a new book bag; on everyone's desk is a brand-new tablet and unsharpened pencils with nice sharp edges on the erasers.

Much of the day goes by in a blur because I'm thinking about getting home to see Jeff. I am not even seriously distracted by the new monkey bars and merry-go-round in the playground.

Finally it's time to get on the school bus to go home. It's a windy, cool day, and we have only a little bit of homework—the usual end-of-summer assignment, which is to write an essay on "What I did this summer." I will write about how Jeff came to live with us. I've already half written it in my head. My book bag isn't heavy. I run all the way in from Brown Hollow Road, and the others straggle along behind me, with Charlie yakking the entire way. I think perhaps Mom will let Jeff out of the basement in time to greet me as I come up the driveway. But there's no sign of him.

I go around to the back door and drop my book bag on the porch.

"I'm home!" I call out. Mom comes into the kitchen. "I'm going down to get Jeff!"

"Wait," Mom says. A funny little wave curls in the pit of my stomach. "Where are Bobby and Charlie and Karen?"

"They're coming," I say. "Did you walk Jeff at noon?"

"Sweetie," she begins, taking my hand. I know what she's going to tell me and I don't want to hear it.

"Let go!" I pull free and run down to the basement, skipping the bottom four steps and falling into the wall, scraping my knee and elbow. Mom follows. I look around quickly, but I already know he isn't there. Mom's worried look tells me that I won't hear Jeff's excited *whuffling* and the *skritching* of his toenails against the floor. But I look just to make sure. I head back up the stairs and nearly collide with my mother, who stands on the landing, blocking my way.

"Daddy took Jeff to that farm over in Tunkhannock this morning," she says, still looking worried.

"He has to go back and get him," I say. "He's my dog. Don't you remember how he came to us? He was meant to be our dog! You said so yourself. He made me stop daydreaming. You didn't even talk to me about this!" Anger makes my voice rise to a squeak.

"This is better for Jeff," Mom says quietly. "You have to think of it that way. If he bit someone, we'd have to put him down. He hates being cooped up in the basement."

"You don't know what he hates!" I say, not caring how unreasonable I sound. I push past her. I run out the door and down to the lake, over to the path that winds through the woods to the pond. I run until I can't breathe, and then fall onto the mossy bank of the stream and cry out my anger. I feel the damp dirt seeping into my white shirt and knee socks, but I don't care. I stay until I'm cold and stiff and it has started to rain.

· I have no choice but to go home. Where else can I go? What good would it do to catch pneumonia—not to mention my father's wrath? It won't bring Jeff back, and that realization starts me crying all over again, so that I walk along with tears and snot dripping off my chin. I wipe my face with the sleeve of my jacket and walk in the rain until I reach the house just as the sun sets, showing a pale glow through the woods.

I close the back door quietly behind me and go into the kitchen without speaking to my mother, who stands at the stove, stirring soup. I go up the stairs to my room, and fling myself onto the bed. My mother comes in quietly a few minutes later and sits on the edge of the bed. She doesn't say anything.

I hope she hollers at me for getting my new clothes dirty so I can holler back. The tears come again, as the realization that Jeff isn't coming back draws over me anew like a suffocating blanket.

"How could you do it?" I try to ask, but I can't get the words out.

"You were too attached to that dog," my mother says. She tries to rub my back, but I turn away.

"Leave me alone!" I say. After a while she gets up and leaves the room, closing the door softly behind her.

Later Karen tiptoes in to tell me dinner is ready. I ignore her and wonder how she can eat, why her world hasn't ended the way mine has. Darkness has begun to settle around the house, so that light from the hallway outside my bedroom reflects from the brass posts of the bed. I hear my father's car in the driveway, and a few minutes later his size 14½ shoes on the steps.

Light from the hallway falls across the bed as he opens the door, and my bed squawks as he sits down on the edge of it. He doesn't say anything, but I won't speak first. I don't even move. He clears his throat.

"You know this is best for Jeff," he says. I don't answer. "He was getting hard to handle. His disposition had turned bad."

"It makes me so sad," I say, my voice shaking and tears burning the backs of my eyes. "He wanted to protect us because he loved us. That was his job! It wasn't that I loved him too much—you took him away because he did his job too well!"

"You'll get over him," my father says.

"I don't want to get over him!" I say, my anger leaking out in pools around the words. We don't talk to my father that way. But I don't care.

"Come down and eat," he says.

"I'm not hungry," I say.

"Come down anyway. And we aren't going to talk about Jeff at the table. Not tonight, not tomorrow. We're not going to talk about him. Understand?" He gets up and leaves the room.

Over the next days I'm mostly aware of my own loss. But I can tell Karen and Bobby are unhappy about Jeff's leaving, too, because of the thin veil of good manners and polite conversation that hangs over the table at mealtimes, where my father insists I present myself even if I don't eat. Nobody mentions Jeff, but his presence is more real than if he were hanging around under the table begging for hand-outs. It's as if everyone is concentrating on not talking about him, on keeping their spirits up—everyone except me.

I can't concentrate in school. I begin to retreat into daydreams. I find one that I can concentrate on. We've been talking about caves in science class. I make an elaborate plan to find a cave and slowly fill it with blankets and pillows and canned goods and matches and pots and cups and plates. And eventually I will go there to live. Then I will find Jeff and bring him back to live with me. I'll take my fishing pole and bait box, and we'll have plenty to eat.

I guard my daydream carefully. I don't tell a soul about it. But one day Mrs. Schwartzstrauber asks my parents to come to school for a talk—a "chat," she says. My father has to sit on Mrs. Schwartzstrauber's chair because there's no way he can fit his knees under a kid's desk.

"Suzanne is present in class," Mrs. Schwartzstrauber says, as if I'm not there. "But she isn't really present—if you know what I mean." She leans forward as she says this, as if she's sharing a secret with my mother and father. She goes on to say that I'm a bright student, but that I won't pass the year if I don't start paying attention in class and doing my homework. She keeps flicking her eyes around the room, passing right over me, as if I'm just an object, like a door or a chair or a desk.

After that my parents change tactics. My father brings home a new fishing pole for me on Saturday. He's bought it on sale at Sugerman's. I thank him and go down to the lake with my new fishing pole, but I end up sitting with it across my knees, my legs dangling out over the water.

I don't even want to play softball when Bobby's friends come in the afternoon. It's a beautiful, warm Indian summer afternoon, the last we can play outdoors in short sleeves until spring. The air is so soft you can feel it touching your arms and face.

For the first time that year I sit out a softball game. I sit on a folding canvas chair and think about how let down Jeff has been by the limitations of human loyalty and love, when his own had been so perfect. It is unspeakably tragic.

By now I've moped about for two weeks, and on Monday my mother lets me stay home from school. She calls Dr. Speicher, who always comes to the house when one of us is sick. Dr. Speicher climbs the stairs to my room to examine me. He's a kindly older man with short gray hair, a small straight mustache, and thick gold-wire-rimmed glasses. My mother sits in the chair beside the window at the head of my bed. He sits on the edge of the bed and listens to my heart, asks me to take several deep breaths, and prods around my stomach.

"You know you have to eat to stay healthy," he says. I nod. "So will you start eating more?"

"I never feel like it," I say. He is writing on a

prescription pad. It's true. I dread mealtimes, with everyone sitting around the table talking about their day. They never even mention Jeff.

Dr. Speicher asks my mother to let him talk to me alone. She gets up without saying anything and leaves the room, closing the door behind her. Thin sunlight shines in through the window at a slant, and for the first time I notice the leaves are turning gold and red on the trees outside. A few dust particles dance around Dr. Speicher's head. He leans forward and looks gravely into my eyes.

"Do you sleep at night?" he asks, and I nod. "Do you dream?" I nod again. "What do you dream about?"

I have to think because I can't always remember. Whenever I tell someone what I've dreamed, they remark that I certainly have odd dreams.

"Strange things," I say.

"Like what?" he asks.

"Well, my mother used to have a blue Cadillac— do you remember it?" He nods. "My father sold that car about three years ago. But I've had maybe four or five dreams that it keeps showing up in our garage. Like a horse that keeps coming back to the barn long after it belongs to someone else."

"Are you afraid of growing up?" he asks. This question surprises me, because I am afraid, and I haven't told anyone—not even myself. I nod slowly.

"Do you know why?" he asks. I shake my head no.

"Do you dream about your dog?" he asks. The answer is no—I haven't dreamed of Jeff at all since he's been gone. But I can't tell him that because hot tears well up in my eyes and my throat closes.

"You might feel as if you'll never get over losing your dog," he says, squeezing my hand. "But you will. And someday you'll grow up to be a fine and productive woman. You'll have a house of your own with room for all the dogs you want."

He talks a little bit more about the importance of eating well and keeping regular habits, and about how some people are unwilling to leave childhood.

"This is pretty normal," he says. "But you have so much to look forward to! You're going to have a wonderful life. And while you're thinking about that, you might also think about the wonderful life Jeff's having on that farm out in Tunkhannock. He's probably chasing ducks on the water right this minute. And tonight he doesn't have to be shut up, because there's no traffic, and nobody to bother him. He's as free as the wind." It's the first thing anyone has said that has made me feel at all better. I nod and smile, and he pats my hand again.

Dr. Speicher rolls down his shirtsleeves and pulls on his jacket. I wait for him to leave the room and go downstairs. Then I get out of bed, put on my slippers and bathrobe, and tiptoe out into the hallway, down to the landing above the foyer. I don't want to miss what he will tell my mother.

"Vitamins," he says, handing my mother the prescription slip. "There's nothing wrong with your daughter that a lot of understanding and a little more time won't cure," he says gently as he puts on his hat and scarf beside the front door. "She has an active imagination, and that might turn out to be a good thing someday." He winks up at where I lie on the landing above the foyer and follows my mother out onto the front porch to say goodbye.

SUZANNE FISHER STAPLES

started her writing career as a news correspondent in Hong Kong, India, and Pakistan. She is the author of many acclaimed books for young readers, including SHIVA'S FIRE, DANGEROUS SKIES, and the Newbery Honor–winning SHABANU: *Daughter of the Wind.* She lives in Chattanooga, Tennessee. You can visit her online at **www.suzannefisherstaples.com**